CAULDRONS CALL
THE CURSE OF THE BLOOD MOON

KRISTEN PROBY

&
AMPERSAND
PUBLISHING, INC.

Cauldrons Call

A Curse of the Blood Moon Novel

By

Kristen Proby

CAULDRONS CALL

A Curse of the Blood Moon Novel

Kristen Proby

Cover Design: By Hang Le

For Kathy

PROLOGUE
GILES COREY

September 1692

"I spoke with your sister three nights past," my dear wife, Martha, says as we sit by the fire. Darkness has fallen outside, and with the accusations swirling around Salem, we are more frightened than ever.

"What did Louisa say?"

"She and her husband will not leave Hallows End. Giles, they are steadfast in their belief that no harm can come to them there."

"No witch is safe in Massachusetts." It comes out as a whisper, in case anyone may hear. "They cannot shield themselves from this hysteria."

"She said they plan to cast the curse."

My head whips up, and I stare at my wife. I love her

with everything in me. Martha and I have only been married for two years, finding each other at our advanced age, after our previous spouses passed. Our children are grown and gone, and she is more precious to me than my wealth or anything else in my possession.

I am an old man. Fighting this war of hysteria is something my body and spirit are almost too weary to withstand.

And yet, for Martha, I will fight with everything I am.

"Louisa suggests we join them in Hallows End, Giles. 'Tis only until this is over, and then we may return home."

"No." I shake my head and stare into the fire once more. "We shall not leave our home. Casting the curse is foolhardy, and Jonas should rethink that decision. There must be another way."

"Jonas is a smart man. An excellent coven leader. Giles, there may not *be* another way."

I sigh, then stand and shuffle to the loose stone in the fireplace. Once I've removed it, I pull out my mother's Book of Shadows.

"*Giles.*" Martha's voice shakes with fear. "You assured me you disposed of that. If someone found it here, we would surely both be hanged."

"Do not be concerned, my love," I reply as I sit and shuffle through the pages until I find the one I want. "I found this today. It is a spell to rewrite history. Martha, this could be what brings all of this to a close without Hallows End disappearing."

"Jonas assured Louisa the curse can be lifted when we are all out of danger."

"And how long might that be?" I demand and drop my fist onto the Book of Shadows. "A year? Five? Martha, I am an old man. I do not want to lose my sister for what remains of my life. At less than thirty and five years, she is still a young woman. And she is all that remains of my family."

"I understand," Martha murmurs, staring into the fire. "I am afraid of losing Louisa, as well."

"Who?" I blink at her, not understanding what she said. "Losing who?"

"I do not know." Martha frowns as if confused. "Why do you have that book out? Giles, someone will harm us if it is found."

I look down and scowl at the book in my lap. Surely, Martha is correct. If anyone saw this, we would indeed be executed.

"I—I do not know."

I stand and return the book to its hiding place.

"We should rest this night, my love. It will be another busy day tomorrow."

CHAPTER ONE
BREENA

"I can do this." I bite my lower lip and grip the small box that just happens to be on the bottom of a pile of *other* packages and give it a pull. Pressing on the ones above in a vain attempt to keep them in place doesn't work, and before I know it, all of them tumble around me. "Shit. I hope nothing broke."

I blow a strand of hair out of my eyes and get to work picking up the mess, but then I bump into *another* stack of boxes, and there's more tumbling.

"For the goddess's sake," I mutter, just as a knock comes from the door. "It's open!"

"Hey there—" my cousin, Lorelei, begins and then stops short. "Are you in there?"

"In the back corner."

"We can't see you over this mountain of *stuff*," comes a reply from my other cousin, Lucy.

The three of us grew up as close as sisters, and I love

that we all live close enough to pop in on one another. At least, I *usually* like it.

"Some boxes fell over." I'm out of breath as I finally retrieve the last package, set it aside, and then stand and smile over at the two people I love the most. "What are you two up to today?"

"We brought coffee," Lorelei says with a frown, looking around the space. "But it looks like we need an intervention here, honey."

I shake my head and scoot around my big craft table, walking to where they are and taking the proffered coffee.

"It's all temporary."

"Listen," Lucy jumps in, "it's awesome that Giles offered to let you use this apartment above his shop so you had a private place to live while you figured out the house situation, but this is *way* too small for you."

"I have a business to run." I shrug, then cringe as I look around the space. "And that business is making things for customers. I need to have the product on hand in order to make said things."

"This is chaos," Lorelei counters with a shake of her head. "And I know you, Breena. You can't take chaos like this for long. It'll drive you crazy."

"It's better than living in that house." A shudder runs through my body at the thought. "And that makes me so mad. I loved that little house. But *it* ruined it for me."

"I don't blame you," Lorelei hurries to assure me, her green eyes full of compassion. "I totally get it. That thing held you prisoner in your own bedroom and tried to *kill* you."

I wince again. "Thanks for the reminder."

"But I told you," she continues as Lucy picks up a candle I've been working on and smells it, "I have plenty of room at my house. You can bring all of this with you."

I shake my head and sip my coffee. "I appreciate the offer. I really do, Lora. But like I told Giles when he tried to get me to move in with him, I need my own space. I think I'm almost ready to put the house on the market anyway. Then it won't matter because I'll have the money from the sale to buy something else."

"Wait." Lorelei holds up a hand. "Giles wants you to move in with him? Like, not just up here but into *his* house?"

I sigh and silently curse myself. Why do I always say stuff I don't mean to? "He mentioned it."

"Like in a friendly way, or in an I-want-to-jump-your-bones-so-come-live-with-me kind of way?" Lucy asks.

"You're incorrigible. Anyway, I'm going to call a realtor and put the house up for sale this week."

"Why haven't you already?" Lucy wants to know. "I'm sure it would sell pretty quickly. Houses in Salem are a hot commodity, and that cottage is adorable."

"Yeah, we just won't tell anyone about the evil entity that attempted to murder the previous owner," Lorelei adds.

"I guess I hoped that maybe I could get past what

happened and move back in." I sigh and move to lean on the table before thinking better of it. "I loved that house. But I don't think that I can ever feel safe there again, and that makes me feel like I'm so weak."

"Not at all," Lucy assures me, shaking her head. "You have nothing to feel weak over. It wasn't your fault."

"*It* attacked you in *your* home, too," I remind her. "And you didn't move out."

"Not in my bedroom," she replies. "And not in the same way. So, you just stop that right now. If you're happy here for now, fine. We won't argue."

"Much," Lorelei adds with a grin. "What are you making today? I love all your creations. You're so freaking creative."

"I found the cutest little crystal teacups at an estate sale," I tell them, getting excited all over again. "A whole set of twelve. I had to have them. So, I brought them back here, cleaned them with soap and water, and then cleansed them with smoke to get any bad energy out. Now, I'm making them into candles for the shop."

"You're so clever at the repurposing thing," Lucy says with a grin. "Are you adding the dried orange slices to them, too?"

"Yes, along with a cinnamon stick and a couple of whole cloves. I think I'll add some crystals, too."

It always makes me so happy when my cousins like what I'm making. They'd say I'm too much of a people pleaser, but I can't help it. It brings me joy. It's my whole purpose in life, and I stopped apologizing for it a long time ago.

"Did you two get a text from Giles this morning?" I ask, trying to sound nonchalant.

"Yeah, he said he found something he wants to show us all later," Lorelei says. "I wonder what it is."

"Knowing Giles, it could be anything." Lucy sniffs another candle. "But he invited us all to *his* house, and that doesn't happen often. We usually meet at Xander's because he has the most space."

"I guess we'll find out in a few hours," I reply. "How's Jonas, Lucy? Anything odd happening lately?"

"No, and he's fine. He says everything in Hallows End has returned to normal—for them, anyway. He goes every morning to walk around town and make sure he's seen. Checks in with everyone. But so far, there's been nothing odd since Samhain."

"Good." I sigh with relief. According to the history of the thing that comes into Salem every year to kill a witch, it only happens in the fall, during Samhain. But I can't shake the feeling that something's still off, despite it being several months later and nearing Beltane.

Spring is here. We should be well out of the time frame of anything sinister happening in Salem. This is the time we should be preparing for the next Samhain so we can defeat it once and for all.

Maybe I just have severe PTSD and need some intense therapy.

But what do I tell them? "*Hey, an evil entity of some*

sort held me prisoner in my bedroom, kept my family and friends away from me, and hung me to death. The ward on the back of my neck brought me back to life."

Yeah, that would go over well.

"You know, I don't want to sound like a broken record here, but you really should consider moving in with Giles," Lorelei says as she continues to survey my space.

"We already covered this."

"Not really. You changed the subject," Lucy replies. "And I agree with her. He has a big place, all to himself, and if he offered..."

I shake my head, but when I turn to walk to the kitchen, another stack of boxes falls.

Truthfully, they're right. I don't thrive in chaos. Every square inch of this tiny one-bedroom apartment is covered in *stuff*. I don't have a living room because I need the space for work. I barely have space in the bedroom for the bed to sleep on.

It's a pain in the ass and makes me feel claustrophobic.

But I don't want to be a burden to anyone.

Ignoring the fallen boxes for now, I continue into the kitchen to fill a pot with water for the stove. However, when I turn the nozzle, nothing comes out.

Spinning, I pin my cousins with a glare.

"I know you're doing this."

"I don't know what you're talking about." Lorelei's eyes are wide with feigned innocence.

"Turn my water back on."

"I don't even have a wrench on me," Lucy says, patting down her pockets and handbag as if looking for one. "It's not us."

"Right." Not giving them the satisfaction of thwarting me, I march over to the fridge and take out a bottle of distilled water. I pour it into the pot and set it on the stove, but nothing happens when I turn on the burner. "Come on, you guys."

"It looks like this place is falling apart." Lorelei turns to Lucy. "I guess she'll just have to move out. But wherever will she go?"

"Hmm." Lucy taps her lips in contemplation, and I cross my arms over my chest, watching them. "I suppose she could move in with Giles. I mean, his house is pretty big for all of her stuff and everything."

"You know, I heard through the grapevine that Giles mentioned that Breena should move in with him. That's *so* convenient."

"*Super* convenient," Lucy agrees with a vigorous nod. "Problem solved."

"Ha ha." I narrow my eyes, glaring at them both. "You're hilarious. You should start your own show or something."

"There is a lot of talent here," Lorelei agrees. "But, alas, the world will just have to miss out on the clever antics of Lora and Lucy. Seriously, though, think about it. Now, enough procrastinating for me. I have to write today, and I've been putting it off all morning."

"How's the book coming along?" I ask. Lorelei spent several years in California teaching folklore at a university, but she came home for good last year, right before all the craziness started.

"It's coming. My publisher wanted to publish it this fall, in time for Halloween, but that's not going to happen. There's too much research involved, and I want to make sure I get it right. So, they pushed it out to next year, which gives me some breathing room. However, that doesn't mean I can pretend like I don't have to do it. So, I'd better get to my desk."

"Thanks for the coffee," I say as I walk them out. Just as we reach the door, the faucet in the kitchen comes on. "And thanks for fixing my sink."

"No idea what you're talking about." Lucy winks.

"I baked cinnamon rolls," I announce as I hold the pan high and walk into Giles's house several hours later. I'm the last to arrive, which is unusual for me. But, well, I didn't want to come.

Which is also not like me.

I've been in love with Giles Corey since I was a little girl. For a long time, I kept it a secret, and then in a moment of weakness when I was nineteen, I confided in Lucy and Lorelei.

But Lorelei spilled the beans last fall. Now, he knows, and I'm still absolutely horrified.

Giles is the kindest man I know, so of *course*, he tried to offer me help. And he's my friend, so he's protective.

But I hate that he feels obligated now because he knows about my crush. I *hate* it. I just wish we could go back to the way things were before.

Not to mention, I absolutely *love* the home Giles moved into about five years ago. It's a big, old house on the edge of town, with a water view, and within walking distance of all my favorite shops and restaurants. So, not only is it in the perfect location, but the house itself is also just dreamy. An old, Puritan-style, two-story home with a white picket fence and a tiny garden in the side yard. It's adorable.

And, yes, it's plenty big for anything I could ever want or need.

But it's not mine. *Giles* isn't mine.

And it's best if I remember that.

"Cinnamon rolls are the best thing in the world any time of day," Lorelei says as Giles takes the pan and smiles down at me.

Gods, he makes my knees weak with that crooked grin and those green eyes behind his black-rimmed glasses. Not to mention how his lips tip up just a bit higher on the left side than the right, and how he smells like pure, unadulterated *male*.

"Thanks," he says with a wink. "I'll get some plates."

"I think you should tell us what you have to say first," Xander, the leader of our coven and a dear friend to us all, chimes in from across the room. Xander is a big, imposing man of close to seven feet tall, with black hair and eyes that can be incredibly disarming—or soothing, depending on his mood.

He's also Lorelei's soulmate.

But he hurt her, and I often wonder if she'll ever let him in again.

From the look on her face right now as she tries her best not to look at him, I'd say the odds of that are slim to none.

"You're right," Giles agrees as I take a seat with the others in the living room. He looks nervous as he sets my pan aside and then rubs the palms of his hands down his jeans. "Okay, to start, I didn't know I had this in my possession. So, first and foremost, I want to sincerely apologize to everyone."

"We are your friends," Jonas reminds him and wraps his arm around his wife's shoulders. "You're safe with us, Giles."

Giles licks his lips and then turns to open a cabinet, pulling out a large, leather-bound book.

"A Book of Shadows," Lorelei says in surprise.

"Yes, from the sixteen hundreds," Giles replies, and I can't help but gasp. "From what I gather, this belonged to the original Giles Corey's *mother*."

"How did you find it?" Xander asks.

"There are a few trunks up in the attic that my mother gave me a couple of years ago when she was downsizing her home," Giles explains. "She called yesterday and asked me if I'd look in them for a photo album she misplaced. When I was digging around, I found this. I had no idea it was upstairs all this time, and I feel like a fool because it might have helped us all along."

"You don't know that for certain," Jonas replies, but his eyes are narrowed on the book. "I knew Giles. He was an old man in the late sixteen hundreds and married to Martha for only a short time then. Louisa, my dear friend in Hallows End, is his sister. She was half his age. His parents had her very late in life, but that wasn't uncommon then."

"Did you know Giles's parents?" I ask Jonas, completely enthralled by this new turn of events.

"No, they were dead by the time I met him, but Louisa told me many times that her mother was a talented and gifted witch. She didn't know where the Book of Shadows was."

"Her brother had it," Giles says. "And it ended up here. I was up all night reading it. Some of the language is a bit foreign to me because English has changed a lot in those hundreds of years, but if I'm reading this right, I think there's a spell we can cast that might just undo everything—including the curse."

"Go on," Xander urges when Giles pauses.

Giles opens the book to a marked page and sits with it, propping it on his lap. "It's something called a Loom of Fate spell. Essentially, we would weave a tapestry with magical textiles and materials, rewriting the history of what happened. Then, when it's finished, we cast a circle and chant the spell, and everything about what happened with Hallows End should be changed."

"That sounds incredibly fanciful, even for me," Lorelei says, speaking up.

"So did a possessed man hanging me in my bedroom," I remind her. "Right now, I'll believe just about anything. *Try* just about anything."

"It certainly can't hurt." Jonas nods. "I don't know what it will mean if we're able to lift the curse that way."

"I think we can write the spell however we choose," Giles says. "We can make it simple and just lift the curse, setting Hallows End free once and for all."

"I can work a loom," I declare with excitement building inside me. "I *have* a loom. Somewhere. I'll need help with the tapestry's design, and we'll have to work together to gather the materials and infuse them with our magic, but this is very doable."

"Where's your loom?" Lucy asks.

"Uh." I blink, thinking. "It's in the guest room of the house, somewhere. I didn't need it, so I didn't bring it to the apartment."

"You can't weave this thing there," Giles says, shaking his head. "It's too big of a project, Breena, and you have no space."

"Interesting," Lorelei adds. "We were *just* having that conversation this morning."

I shoot her a look, but Lorelei only smiles at me.

"I can make it work."

"Might I suggest," Xander starts, those piercing black

eyes on me, "that you take Giles up on his offer and come stay here for the time being while we work through this project, at least?"

"It makes sense," Lucy adds, her voice soft as she smiles at me. "You have to agree that the space you have now is simply inadequate, Breena."

I blow out a breath and glance over at Giles, who watches me with those somber eyes. I really don't want to make anything more uncomfortable than it already is.

I don't want to be more embarrassed than I already am.

"Maybe I can just move back into my house."

"No. Absolutely not."

CHAPTER TWO
GILES

Five pairs of eyes whip over to me, but I don't take my gaze off Breena. Anger moves through my veins, hotter than it has in a long time.

"What?" Breena asks, frowning at me.

"You won't go live in that house." I shake my head and cross my arms over my chest, absolutely unwilling to waver on the point. "It terrifies you, Breena. It's not going to stop just because you have a new project to work on."

She casts her gaze down, and I feel like an asshole for making her uncomfortable. But damn it, she's so fucking stubborn, and it drives me out of my mind.

"I think I'm overreacting." Her voice is smaller now, and Lorelei shoots me a look that would make a weaker man wither and fall through the floor.

"You're not." I walk to Breena, take her hand in mine, and link our fingers, immediately feeling her relax.

"You're not overreacting at all. What happened to you—to all of us—in that house was terrifying, and it makes sense that you don't want to stay there. Breena, I have more room than I know what to do with here. You can spread out, take it over. I won't mind a bit."

She nibbles on her bottom lip, and I can't help but think what a blind idiot I was for not seeing that she had feelings for me for so long. She's always been my friend, and part of me always wanted more, but she's younger than me, and I didn't think I'd ever have a chance in hell.

"I think it's the right thing to do," Lucy asserts. When Breena looks over at her, her cousin nods in encouragement. "It'll feel good to be out of that cramped space, Breena."

Finally, Breena sighs and looks at me. "You mean it when you say you don't mind? You're not just saying it to be kind?"

"I wouldn't lie about that. If I didn't want you here, I'd say so."

She licks her lips and seems to make up her mind because she abruptly stands.

"I guess I'd better start packing, then."

"We can help," Xander offers, but Breena shakes her head.

"I appreciate it, and maybe when it's time to actually move the stuff over, I can use the extra hands, but I'm kind of particular about how I want things packed. I cast little spells and set intentions."

"I understand," Xander says. "Thank you for stepping outside your comfort zone to help us, Breena."

She seems to think something over and then looks around the room, tears filling her eyes.

"Honey, what is it?" Lorelei asks.

"I love you all so much." Breena swallows hard. "The last thing I want is to be a burden on anyone."

Unable to stop myself, I loop an arm around her shoulders, and Breena immediately rests her head against me.

"No one in this room is a burden," I say softly. "At the very core of it all, we're friends, Breena. Always have been. You're *always* welcome in my home, and that will never change."

She nods and seems to pull herself together, squaring her shoulders. "Okay. Thank you. I have so much to do. I really should be going."

"I have more research to do now that we know about this spell," Xander says as he stands. "But I won't pass up one of Breena's cinnamon rolls."

"Oh, that's right." Breena laughs. "I forgot all about them."

"Trust me," Lucy says, "none of us forgot. They smell amazing."

"Let's eat too much sugar and enjoy each other before we get back to the heavy stuff," Lorelei suggests. "We deserve it."

I t's been three days since the meeting at my home when I finally talked Breena into coming to stay with me. Once I close the shop for the day, I'll move her in.

I wish she would've come to live in the house when everything started. I want her nearby, where I know she's safe.

But I also understand her need for privacy and independence.

It's one of the things I love about her.

But I've been counting the minutes until I can close the shop and roll up my sleeves to get Breena settled at the house.

I recheck the clock and feel my heartbeats quicken. Only ten minutes left until closing time.

Grabbing my duster, I make my way around the shop, sweeping away anything that's settled on my large pieces of crystal and petrified wood. Some are for sale, and others are showpieces I'll never sell.

Particularly a huge piece of labradorite handed down through my family for generations, ever since the time of Giles Corey in the sixteen hundreds. It will never leave my collection, but I love displaying it in my shop. It's flashy and beautiful, and it often inspires customers to buy smaller pieces of the same crystal.

I rub my hand down its smooth surface before moving to the next, hearing the bell above the door ring as someone walks in.

I glance over and smile at Jeremy Cousins, a long-time customer and friend.

"Hey there," I say, catching his attention.

"Hi, Giles. I'm glad I caught you before you closed. I need a gift for my wife, and I'm stuck."

"What's the occasion?"

"Last day of chemo." Jeremy's eyes soften as he glances my way. "It's been a long haul, and she deserves something pretty."

"She absolutely does. Do you want jewelry? Crystals? Or both?"

"I'm open to ideas. She's at her last appointment now, so I thought I'd swing in here and then meet her at the hospital so I can be there when she rings the bell."

"We've got this," I assure him. "I have an idea. What if we put together a gift set of crystals with healing properties and also find her a beautiful piece of jewelry?"

"I think that sounds great," Jeremy replies. "She wears the hematite bracelet you gave her at the last coven meeting all the time. She swears by it."

"So do I." I grab a velvet-lined tray and set out to intuitively choose some stones for Maggie, placing them inside. "I'm also going to grab some rose quartz, amethyst, kunzite, and clear quartz."

When I've finished, and we approach the counter, I set the tray aside, and we dig in to find the perfect piece of jewelry.

"We won't have children," Jeremy says softly. "After her surgery...well, it's not possible."

"I'm sorry." I reach over and pat my friend's shoulder, feeling the anguish, worry, and fear running through him. "But Maggie will be okay?"

"They say she has an excellent chance of complete recovery without the cancer coming back."

"That's amazing news." I push my glasses up the bridge of my nose. "I'm not a father either, Jeremy. But here's something to think about. There's more than one way to add children to your family."

He nods and seems to relax. "I know. I know it. We just had these big plans, you know? And it's all changed."

"I think you'll make it through this as long as you have each other. What do you think of an emerald necklace?"

I pull out the pendant that hangs from a long, gold chain.

"That's gorgeous, Giles, but I'm quite sure I can't afford it."

"You can." I hold it up higher. "I'm giving you the friends-and-family discount on this one. Consider it a congratulatory gift from a friend."

Jeremy blows out a breath and stares at the emerald. "If you're sure, I'll take it. She'll love it."

"Good."

I get everything wrapped for him and then walk him to the door.

"Give Maggie my love. When she's feeling up to it, the coven should meet for a celebration."

"We'd enjoy that." Jeremy shakes my hand. "Thank you."

"You're welcome."

I watch him walk through the rain to his car, then lock the door and turn the sign to *Closed*.

I can hear Breena upstairs, walking back and forth, probably packing up the last of her boxes, so I hurry to close everything down for the night and then head up the stairs to the apartment.

The door is already open.

"Hello?"

"In the kitchen," Breena calls out. "I just have to box up the fridge stuff; everything else is ready to go."

"You could have left some stuff for me to do," I remind her and make my way through the maze of boxes stacked six feet high to the kitchen. "Xander's pulling up with the moving truck now."

"Lucy just texted," Breena says with a smile. "They're on their way. It shouldn't take long with everyone pitching in."

My tongue is suddenly stuck to the roof of my mouth. Goddess, she's beautiful. Her thick, blonde hair is pulled up in a wispy bun with tendrils framing her face. Her lips are plump and pink from biting them all day, which is what she always does when she's nervous or busy.

And the T-shirt and denim shorts she's wearing hug every curve perfectly.

I've always known that Breena is a beautiful woman.

Something inside me has always longed for her. But over the past six months, I've grown to crave her in a way I never expected.

"Giles?"

I blink, clearing my head. "I'm sorry, what?"

"I said I think I hear people on the stairs."

"Oh, right. I'll go greet them, and we'll get this show on the road."

It takes us less than two hours to load all of Breena's things, drive them to my house, and unpack the truck.

Before I can even offer the others something to eat, they all wish us well and take off again.

Breena and I stand in the foyer of my house, surrounded by boxes, staring at each other.

"Now what?" she asks with a nervous little laugh.

"Well, I think I should give you a tour before we start trying to make sense of all of this." I gesture around the space.

"Good idea." She brushes at the hair on her cheek. "I've always wanted a tour of this house."

"You have?" I turn to her in surprise. "Why didn't you just ask for one?"

"I don't know. I guess that seemed...rude."

"It's not rude at all. Okay, let's start upstairs and work our way down, shall we?"

"We shall." She grins as she follows me to the stairs. "What's the history?"

"It was originally built in the early eighteen hundreds," I begin. When we get to the top of the stairs,

I gesture for her to follow me down the hall. "The original building burned down about a hundred years ago and was rebuilt, so this structure isn't that old."

"I mean, a hundred years is still pretty old."

"True, but not compared to so many other homes in the area. But that's also good because it's more modern-looking, even though it's still Puritan style. There are three bedrooms and two bathrooms up here. My room is at the end of the hallway, that way." I point. "Yours is on the opposite side of the house to give you more privacy."

I glance down at her and catch her biting her lip.

"I hope that's okay."

"Of course. It's your house, Giles, I'm happy to sleep anywhere."

I lead her down the hall and open the door to her room. "There's an attached bathroom, so you won't have to share with me, and there's even a view of the garden. I thought you'd like that."

"I really do love that little garden," she murmurs as she walks inside and takes in the queen-sized bed and simple furnishings. "It's lovely."

"It's simple, but I know you'll make it your own. I want you to feel at home here, Breena."

"Thank you."

With that, I lead her to another guest room and open the door. "I had the bed and furniture removed from this space, thinking you could use it for a craft area, or maybe you can put the loom in here."

"Is there room downstairs for crafts?" she asks, thinking it over.

"Yes, I'll show it to you."

"Then I'll probably use this room for the loom. It's easier."

I nod, and we make our way back downstairs.

"I *adore* your kitchen," she says as we walk through the mudroom to the kitchen. "You have so much counter space, and that stove is just to *die* for."

"It's all yours."

She whips around to face me with wide eyes.

"I'm serious. I don't cook here much except to pour myself some cereal in the morning before work. You can use everything here. For whatever you need."

"I'll take you up on that."

"I hope so. Come on, this is the best part."

Around the corner is a glassed-in room I think is perfect for her.

"A sunroom."

"Yes, but it could also work for a craft room. It's plenty big enough for the worktable, and we can add shelves for all your supplies. I also have blinds that will cut some of the direct sunlight."

"It really is perfect. Thank you, Giles. But what did you do with all the furniture?"

"What furniture?" I laugh and turn to her. "I've never had anything in this room. It just sits here."

"Well, that's a waste."

"Not anymore."

A door slams upstairs, and Breena raises an eyebrow.

"Ah, yes, that's Molly."

"Who's Molly?"

"My house ghost."

I turn to walk away, but Breena catches my arm to stop me.

"Whoa. Tell me more about that. Who is she? How long has she been here?"

"I'm not a medium," I remind her. "I can't speak with her, but I know she's been here for a long time. I did a little research after she made herself known when I moved in. Molly Adams died in the fire, and she's still here. She's harmless. I think she likes me because she pretty much leaves me alone. Sometimes, she'll move things around, and she likes to slam doors occasionally, which isn't convenient at three o'clock in the morning. But, otherwise, it's not a big deal."

"Interesting," Breena says. "Was she the only casualty in the fire?"

"As far as I know, yes."

"Maybe Lorelei can talk to her sometime." Breena turns from me. "Hi, Molly. I'm Breena. I'll be staying here for a little while. I'm not here to hurt or upset you. I hope we can be friends."

A light in the kitchen comes on, and Breena smiles.

"Yes, I'd love to hang out with you in your kitchen."

The light goes out, and Breena turns back to me.

"I think Molly and I will be just fine."

Unable to help myself, I brush the hair from Breena's

cheek, hooking it behind her ear. "Do you have any idea how sweet you are?"

"I'm not—"

"Yes. You are. You care enough to make nice with a ghost. I'm glad you're here, and I won't make things weird or awkward for you, but I think it's time you know something."

Her gaze dips to my lips, and it takes everything in me not to kiss her right here in the sunroom.

"What's that?"

"When Lorelei spilled the tea all those months ago about how you've had a crush on me for years, and I seemed surprised and acted like a complete moron, it wasn't because I was upset or put off by the idea."

She starts to move away, discomfited by the direction of the conversation, but I take her hand and keep her where she is.

"It's okay, Giles. It was just a teenage crush, nothing to worry about."

"I *was* surprised," I continue, ignoring her comment, "but because I've watched and wanted you for a long damn time. We were always squarely in the friend zone, though. Our families know each other. We're in the same coven... We're *friends*. I didn't want to fuck that up by trying to hit on or date you because if it fell flat, I knew I'd probably lose you, and that's not a possibility for me."

Breena's jaw drops, and her green eyes go wide.

"And it upset me that you had the same feelings for

me all that time, and we could have been together. We could have tried."

She finally finds her voice. "But as you said, if it doesn't work, we'll lose each other. What we're working on right now is too important, Giles. We *need* to work together."

I nod because I agree with her.

"I don't want you to think that *you* aren't just as important, Breena. Because you are. And I'm really sick and tired of you being embarrassed and avoiding me over something you shouldn't be ashamed of or self-conscious about."

"Why didn't you say something before?"

I shrug and take a small step back before I do something silly like push her against the wall to have my way with her.

"As I said, you've been avoiding me like the plague. You haven't given me much chance to spill my guts to you."

Breena blows out a breath and crosses her arms over her chest.

"So, you're telling me my crush wasn't one-sided?"

"That's what I'm telling you."

"And what does that mean now?"

I shrug and push my hand through my hair. "It doesn't have to mean anything right now. I just thought you should know. We can be embarrassed together."

Her lips tip up in that sweet smile I love so much.

"Okay. I guess the first thing I need to do is unpack

so I can get ready to weave a tapestry—which is not something I thought I'd ever say."

"If anyone can do it, it's you." Unable to resist, I push that stubborn lock of hair behind her ear once more. Breena takes a little step toward me and tips her face up as if in invitation.

I lean in and brush my lips over her cheek, then move down to her ear.

"I'm going to take things one step at a time, Breen. I'm not going to mess this up."

CHAPTER THREE
BREENA

I t's taken me a week, but I'm finished unpacking. After breaking down the last box and setting it neatly on the back porch the way Giles asked so he could take care of the recycling, I rest my hands on my hips and survey the kitchen.

It was a barren space a week ago, with no homey touches on the countertops, and nothing simmering on the stove. Instead, it was simply a pretty kitchen. It could have graced the pages of a magazine, but it had no character.

"I think we've changed that," I murmur with a happy sigh. My big cast-iron pot is on the stove, ready for my next simmer pot. I have bottles of herbs and jars of this and that arranged just so on the counter, and I recently took my first loaf of rosemary bread out of the oven.

Having a big kitchen to create in was something I missed more than anything when I was in the apartment.

I *love* to bake, cook, and imagine things in spaces like this. And now, because of Giles's generosity, I can dig back into that stuff.

The former sunroom is now organized, with my big craft table in the center of the room, the shelves lined with products so I can make my creations for my business, and all my posters of beautiful botanicals and animals adorning the walls.

My bedroom is ready to go upstairs, with a quilt my grandmother made on the soft bed and all my clothes organized in the closet.

The only thing left to do is return to my cottage to fetch the loom so I can get going on the tapestry spell.

Giles has been working in his office all morning, so I don't bother to interrupt him. I just write a little note on a sticky and set it on the countertop.

Giles-

Ran an errand. Back soon.

-B

Going back to the cottage terrifies me, and that makes me so dang mad. It used to be my sanctuary. Now, I can't stand the thought of stepping foot inside it. But the loom is there, along with some of my supplies, and I have to get them—I can't put it off any longer.

So, with my bag and keys in hand, I walk down to my car and climb inside. But unfortunately, when I turn the key, nothing happens.

It's just...*dead.*

"Are you kidding me right now?" I mutter and glare

at the steering wheel. "I just had you tuned up last month, and you had a clean bill of health. Come on, start for me."

I try the key again with no luck.

"I can't walk over there and carry the loom back," I whine as I step out of the car and give the tire a good kick.

I guess I'll have to interrupt Giles, after all.

I find him at his desk, reading something on his computer, his glasses drooping on the bridge of his nose.

"Hey," I say softly. He turns to me, and I cringe. "Sorry to interrupt. My car won't start."

He pushes the glasses up his nose and stands. "I needed the interruption. I've been reading for so long I think I'm going cross-eyed. Let's go check it out."

"Thanks."

Giles follows me out to my car, and I gesture at the pile of rusty bolts that's trying to pass off for an automobile.

"I just had it tuned up, but it won't start. I turn the key, and *nothing*."

"I can give you a ride if we can't figure it out. Where were you headed?"

"I have to go to the cottage to get the loom."

Giles freezes with the car door open and turns to scowl at me. "You're absolutely *not* going to the cottage alone, Breena."

"It's fine. Whatever was there is long gone. It's just a house, Giles. No big deal at all."

"No." He shakes his head emphatically. "Absolutely not."

"Do you always tell women what to do?"

"Only when they're being ridiculous, and I care about their safety," he quips, his voice completely calm and mild. "You were terrorized in that house, Breena. I'll go with you to get the loom."

He tries to start the engine, and it purrs right to life.

"Hey!"

"See? Even the universe is telling you not to go by yourself," he says as he steps out. But he doesn't go back to the house. No. Instead, he circles the car and climbs into the passenger seat. "Let's go."

"Are you going to lock the house?"

With a smug smile on his sexy lips, he waves his hand. "Done."

I sigh as I lower myself into the driver's seat. "You were busy, Giles."

"Not too busy. This won't take long."

Resolved to having him with me, I pull out of his driveway and head to the other side of town, where my cottage sits.

"It really is in a great spot," I whisper as it comes into view. "On the edge of town, not much foot traffic, hidden back in the trees."

"It's a great spot. A great house," he confirms and reaches over to take my hand, giving it an encouraging squeeze. "I'm sorry, sweetheart."

I park and take a deep breath, allowing myself to feel

sad that I lost my sweet home because of something horrible.

"The next place will be great, too." I glance his way and offer him a bright, fake smile. "It'll be fine. It's just a house."

"Right." He kisses my hand and then lets it go, but I feel the touch all the way to my toes. It's *electric* how he lingers in my body, even after he's gone. "Just a house. Let's get this over with, okay?"

I nod and open my car door, immediately feeling it. The energy, even though it's gone, created such an indelible mark on the area that I can hardly breathe as I approach the house.

"Do you feel that?" I ask Giles.

"Yeah. Here." He retakes my hand and presses a big chunk of black tourmaline into my palm. "Do not, under any circumstances, put that down. I cast a special protection spell on it just for you."

I smile up at him, delighted that he would go out of his way to do that for me. "That's so sweet."

"And necessary." His lips are tight, his expression grim as I turn to unlock the front door.

I haven't been back here in more than five months, not since the day after everything went down. My family and friends were kind enough to pack everything I needed and bring it to me.

I left the rest behind.

When I open the door, the air rushes out and over me.

Through me.

"Well, that was creepy," I mutter as I walk inside, immediately beginning a protection spell. "*Only love and light are welcome here. Only that which serves us in our highest good may stay.*"

I continue saying it over and over as I wander through the house.

"I need my sewing basket," I say to Giles. "It's over there by the chair in the living room."

"Got it." His eyes never stop moving over the space. It's as if he's staying alert in case something tries to jump out and get us.

I point out a few more things I want to be sure to take with me, and then we move to the guest room where the loom is.

"Did you just see a shadow move across the hallway?" I ask as I stop in my tracks.

"We won't speak of it," he says, his voice low. "Let's get the fucking loom and get out of here."

"Okay." I open the guest room door, but the loom isn't in the corner where I left it. "It's been sitting right over there for years, Giles. It was handed down in my family for generations."

"Maybe you moved it to the attic to make room for something else in here?"

"I hate the attic. It's cobwebby and dark and just...*no.*"

"Let's check anyway."

"You can check. I'm not climbing that ladder."

He grins and nudges me with his shoulder. "Okay, I'll climb."

With the ladder pulled down from the ceiling, Giles climbs it until his head and shoulders disappear, then he turns on his phone's flashlight.

"You're right. There's not much up here except spiders."

I scrunch up my nose and shiver. "Ew."

"I'm coming down."

He pushes the ladder back into the ceiling and sighs.

"Maybe my mom came to get it," I say, thinking it over. "I'll call her."

But when I pull my phone out of my pocket, the battery is dead.

"How is that possible? It was full when we left."

"Lots of energy in this house," he intones softly, his eyes saying *we won't discuss this here.*

"Let's just go back to your place. I'll buy a new loom, I guess."

But when we walk past the guest room, there it is, in the corner, exactly where it's been for a long, long time.

"I've got it," Giles says grimly, walking in to pick it up. "Now, let's get the fuck out of here."

"I'm with you."

Once outside, and after I've locked up, I turn to Giles and put my hand on his arm.

"You can't put that in the car until I cleanse it out here first. I won't take any bad energy home with us."

He nods and sets the loom on the ground. I place my sewing basket next to it and then take Giles's hand.

Witches are stronger in numbers.

"Only love and light may stay. Anything not here for our highest good must go away."

I cast the spell and raise my hands, putting the force of everything I know and the knowledge of my ancestors into the working. I won't risk Giles's safety by bringing something sinister into his home.

Suddenly, little sparks fire into the air around my items. Tiny flames dance, burn blue, and then disappear.

The air pulses around us as the wind picks up, seeming to sweep through the items, cleansing them with my words.

Finally, when I've finished the spell, the air swirls up and away, leaving us in the stillness with my things once more.

"Holy shit," Giles says, staring down at me. "You're one powerful witch, Breena."

"I have my moments. Come on. I want to get out of here."

We load the items into my car and immediately drive away. I don't even look in the rearview mirror, afraid of what I might see.

"No, you won't be going back there," Giles says softly.

"Maybe to cleanse it," I reply. "But never to live. And I'm not nearly as sad about that as I was when we arrived."

"You need me." Those are the first words out of my mom's mouth when I open the door to her the next morning. I can't help but rush into her arms and hug her close, so relieved to see her.

"I always need you, Mama."

"I suspect you're behind in your work, what with everything going on, and I came to help out."

"You must have been reading my mind." I close the door behind her and lead her back to the kitchen. "I'm making Beltane candles for our coven celebration in a couple of weeks, and I need to make some extras to sell on my site."

"I love making candles," Mama says as she reaches for the apron I offer her. "You always add the best oils."

"Lucy makes them in her apothecary," I inform her with a smile. "She's so talented."

"All our girls are talented," Mama insists. "What else are you making for Beltane?"

"All kinds of things. Come into the craft room, and I'll show you."

"Oh, my goddess," Mama murmurs when we walk into the former sunroom. "Breena, this is beautiful."

"I know. It's kind of a dream, honestly. It's the perfect workspace for my crafts. It'll be hard to leave it when the time comes to buy another house."

"Hmm," is all she says.

"We went to get the loom," I tell her. "Giles went with me, thank the gods. There's still some scary stuff happening over there, Mom."

"What kind of scary stuff?" she asks, frowning at me. "The energy left."

"Yeah, but I think it opened a doorway of some kind." I swallow hard. "There were shadows, *really* icky energy, and...it's just not my place anymore. That makes me so mad because that house was my sanctuary. It was my *home*. I created there, dreamed there, and I planned to live there for a very long time. All that was taken from me. I know it could be so much worse and *would* have been if not for the ward on my neck."

I reach back to rub my hand over my nape where the tattoo is.

"But damn it, it took my home."

"And it's perfectly natural to grieve for it," Mama says as she busies herself preparing wicks for the candles. "You know, we need to bring the coven together to cleanse that house before you try to sell it. You can't put it on the market as it is."

"No, I know. I was going to ask everyone at Beltane if they'd help me with it. I can't afford to keep it, but I can't in good conscience pawn it off on someone the way it is either. It'll have to be torn down if we can't purify it."

"I think we can cleanse it well enough for someone," Mama says. "It'll be okay, pumpkin."

I grin at her. "Aren't I too old to be called *pumpkin*?"

"Never."

"You know, I think I'll make us some tea for while we work."

I turn toward the little coffee and tea bar I set up in one of the kitchen's nooks, and before I can walk over there, the light above the station flips on.

"Is someone here with us?" Mama asks.

"Yeah, that's Molly. She's the resident ghost, but she's a good one. She's been really friendly."

"Fascinating," my mom replies. "You're having all kinds of new experiences in this house, Breena."

"No kidding." I set the pot on the stove and ready the cups, the tea bags, and the honey. When the water boils, I pour it, then get the spoons stirring.

On their own.

"You've always been good at that spell," Mama says as I pass her a mug.

"You and the aunts taught us when we were little. I think it was the first magical working we ever did."

"It's a simple one." She shrugs and takes a sip.

The light above the station goes out.

"She's a helpful ghost."

I grin. "Yes, she is. I think she likes me."

"What's not to like?"

"**T**hanks for coming today." Several hours later, I walk Mama to the door. "I needed it."

"I'm sorry we didn't get more done, but we were too swept up in gossip."

I laugh and hug her close. "It's okay. Sometimes, that's all you need to accomplish in one day—spending time with your mom."

She frames my face in her hands. "I love you, sweet girl. You're safe here."

"I know. I feel it."

I open the door for her and see Giles just pulling into the driveway.

"Oh, good, I get to say hello to Giles."

I wait on the porch as Mama walks down to her car and says hello to the man I'm currently living with.

He smiles happily when he sees her, his whole face lighting up in welcome, then plucks a pink rose out of the bouquet in his hand and offers it to her.

To her utter delight.

He's a handsome man, so tall, broad, and strong. But his brain has always fascinated me the most.

He's just so *smart*.

When he kisses my mom on the cheek and then turns to walk up the steps to me, the twinkle in his eyes makes me weak in the knees.

"I brought these for you." He offers me the flowers. I accept them before waving to my mother.

"You've brought something home to me every day

this week." I bury my nose in a blossom to fuss over it a little. "Yesterday, it was my favorite coffee. Today, it's flowers. Are you trying to romance me or something?"

"Well, look at that." He leans in to kiss my cheek. "She's finally catching on."

I laugh and lead Giles into the house and back to the kitchen so I can put the flowers into a vase with some water.

"My mom came and spent the day with me. She wanted to help me get caught up with work, but we didn't get much done. We mostly just talked all day."

"That's accomplishing something." He smiles. "She looks good."

"I think she's doing well. It's been tough on her and Astrid since Aunt Agatha died, but they're recovering."

"It's good that they have each other," he says.

"How are your parents? I haven't seen them in a while."

"They've been in Philadelphia, visiting my dad's family. Unfortunately, his father's been ill."

"Oh, I'm sorry to hear that."

"I think they plan to come home in time for Beltane. It's Mom's favorite holiday."

"I love it, too. The mid-point between the spring equinox and summer solstice, and how everything is getting so green. So much promise in that."

"That's what she always says."

He grins, and his gaze falls to my lips.

Goddess, I want him to kiss me more than I want just about anything else.

As if he can read my mind, he steps a little closer and reaches out to glide his hand across my hip. Just as his face lowers, right before those lips press over mine, my phone rings.

"Don't answer it," he urges softly. "They'll call back."

"Good idea."

The kiss is everything I've dreamed of for *years*. Soft and sweet, yet just a little demanding and confident.

Giles *wants* me.

I don't have to be sensitive to feel it coming off him in waves.

And it's the best thing I've ever felt in this or any lifetime.

"You're so fucking sweet." His breath is hot as he rests his forehead against mine.

"I was thinking the same about you."

He pulls back and lifts an eyebrow. "*Sweet?*"

"Oh, yeah. Along with some other things."

"Let's talk about those other things."

Chapter Four
Giles

Breena's phone rings again, pulling us out of the sexy intoxication we're in and dropping us right back into reality.

"I'd better get that," she says apologetically with a smile before pulling away to reach for her cell.

I feel the loss of her all the way to the marrow of my bones, which is ridiculous because she's *right here*. But my need for her grows every day she's in my house. The need to protect her. The need to touch her.

The need to fucking *love* her. I won't even get into the desperate need to take her to my bed and make her mine in every way possible.

It all seems to be moving so fast; I feel like I'm in hyperdrive. But I also don't want it to stop. Because until Breena came to stay here, I felt like I was living in black and white. The moment she walked through the front door, she cast my entire world into vivid color and brought *life* into my house.

My phone rings, and I leave the room to answer it.

"This is Giles."

"You're so professional."

I grin at my mother's voice. "Well, hello there. I didn't even look at the caller ID. How's it going in Pennsylvania?"

"Better, actually. Harry's starting to feel better, much to everyone's surprise, so your father and I are coming home tomorrow. I need to tend to my gardens and get ready for Beltane. How are you? I sense stuff going on, but I can't put my finger on it."

I hear Breena laughing in the other room and let out a long breath. "A lot has been going on, actually."

"Are you safe?"

My parents' fear has been palpable since Samhain and everything that happened with the evil entity that's hell-bent on killing us.

And almost succeeded with one of us.

"Yes, I'm safe. Breena's staying with me for a while, and we've come up with a new idea to hopefully break the curse on Hallows End."

"Well, I can't wait to hear about everything."

"Why don't you and Dad come over for dinner on Friday?"

"That sounds perfect. I'll see you then. Stay safe, son. Blessed be."

"I love you."

I hang up and take a deep breath. I'm glad they're coming home. I've had a niggling feeling in the back of my head since they left town, something telling me they shouldn't have gone.

Having them back in Salem will make me feel better.

"Who was that?" Breena asks as she walks into my office. Suddenly, her eyes widen, and she claps her hand over her mouth. "I'm *so* sorry. That's none of my business."

"It was my mother," I reply easily, shoving my hands into my pockets so I don't reach for her again. "They're returning from Philly and coming here for dinner on Friday."

"Oh, that's great. I'll go hang out with Lorelei while they're here."

"Why would you do that?" I lean on the desk and tip my head to the side. "You don't have to go anywhere, Breena. You're living here. Besides, my mom will be upset if she doesn't get to see you."

"I really do love your mom," Breena admits softly. "And I wanted to ask her for a recipe."

"Perfect, then. Who were *you* chatting with?"

"Oh." Her cheeks flush, and she waves me off. "It was nothing."

"Who was on the phone, Breena?"

She worries her lower lip and then sighs.

"Hey. Why don't you want to tell me?"

"Because it was a man, but I don't want you to get the wrong idea, and I don't even know why I'm worried about that, but I am because I don't want to hurt your feelings, even though there would be no reason for your feelings to be hurt in the first place, but I'm a pleaser, and it makes me worry."

"Whoa. You sure talk fast when you're nervous." Unable to stop myself, I cross to her and take her shoulders in my hands. "You don't have to explain yourself to me or anyone. If you're dating someone, and I didn't realize it, I apologize for the kiss earlier."

"No." Her eyes widen, and she shakes her head emphatically. "No, that's not it at all. For Hades' sake, I've only had eyes for *you* my entire adult life. And I can't believe I just said that. I think I'll just go upstairs and hide under the bed."

"Hold on." I chuckle and wrap my arms around her, holding on tight. "Before we both want to disappear from embarrassment, let's just take a deep breath."

She does just that, breathes in deeply, and lets the air out slowly. Then, she returns my hug, wrapping her arms around my waist and planting her hands on the middle of my back, holding on.

"Let's go back to the beginning," I suggest softly and kiss the top of her head. "My parents will be here on Friday for dinner. I hope you'll join us."

"Thanks, I'd like that." Her voice is soft, and she still has her face buried in my chest.

"What do you have planned for the rest of the evening?"

Her head whips up at my question, and she looks completely surprised. "I was talking to Lad Iverson."

"Okay." Lad's a businessman in Salem. He's single and young, and I've heard the women call him *hot*. But I know without a shadow of a doubt that Breena isn't interested in him. "I hope he's well."

"He is. He just wanted to buy some stuff for his sister, Merrilee, who recently joined the coven. She's new, and he's not at all on our path, but he wants to support her and buy her something nice for her birthday. So, he reached out to me."

"He definitely called the right person." I brush my finger down her soft cheek. "Sweetheart, I'm not mad. I mean, did you have phone sex with him or something right after I kissed you?"

That makes her snort. "Definitely not."

"Then I think everything's just fine."

"He did ask me out to dinner."

I still and watch her closely, remaining quiet. Her brows furrow, but she doesn't drop her gaze from mine.

"Okay. And what did you say?"

"I thanked him but turned him down, of course."

"Why would you think that would hurt my feelings?"

She blows out a breath and leans her forehead against my chest once more. "I don't know. I have to stop doing this. I'm always so worried about how other people feel that I just walk on eggshells all the freaking time. And I'm so tired, Giles. It's exhausting."

I simply take her hand and lead her to the sofa, then sit and tug her down onto my lap.

"Come here." I settle in and grin at her. "This is kind of nice, isn't it?"

"Actually, yes. It is."

"Good, we'll do this more often. Okay, I have some things to say, and I'm your friend first, always, so remember that, all right?"

"Just tell me."

She closes her eyes, clearly readying herself for the worst. It makes my heart ache for her.

"You're the most amazing person I've ever met."

Her eyes spring open. "Huh?"

"You heard me. I don't know what happened to you before that made you feel like you have to make everybody happy all the time. Whatever it was clearly put fear in you about what will happen if you don't. But I won't be an asshole and tell you to just stop it."

"Thanks, because I've tried."

"I'm sure you have." I kiss her forehead. "I can say this, though. You don't have to walk on eggshells around *me*. Not ever. I'm not quick to anger, and I don't expect anything from you, Breena. Just your friendship and kindness, and that's pretty much a no-brainer for you."

"I think I'm confused," she admits and bites her lip again.

"Now, we're getting somewhere. What are you confused about?"

"Well, *before*, when Lorelei was an idiot and spilled

the tea about my crush on you, you seemed completely horrified."

"No, I—"

She gently presses her fingertips against my lips, effectively shutting me up.

"And then you wanted to talk about it, and we did. But I still avoided you because I was embarrassed."

All I can do is nod.

"*Then*, you told me you had a crush on me, too. And you kissed me. And you've been so sweet to me."

"But?" I ask against her fingers.

"I...I don't know. What's going on between us, Giles? Because if it's just friendly flirtation and stuff, I need to know."

I take her hand and kiss it, then press it to my chest so I can reply.

"I don't usually kiss my friends like I kissed you earlier. And I don't bring them flowers. I don't think about them all damn day when I'm at work, and, well... You get the idea."

She simply watches me with those gorgeous eyes.

"I'm glad you don't want to go to dinner with Lad. Because if anyone's going to take you out on dates, I'd like it to be me. I know we have a lot on our plates with a three-hundred-year-old curse to lift and a homicidal supernatural maniac to find, and I don't want to pressure you into anything too fast, but I—"

Goddess, now what do I say? *I love you*? *I need you*? *I*

want you with me forever? I've known her for most of her life. But this? This feels like a lot.

"I get it," she says and smiles. "And I think we're on the same page."

"Well, good."

"As long as you don't plan on seeing anyone else either."

I laugh and lean in to breathe her in. "Sweetheart, you're all I see."

Suddenly, a door slams upstairs, startling us both.

"Maybe Molly's jealous," Breena whispers, but her fingers shake as she reaches for me.

"Hmm." I cock my head and listen. I don't know why, but that didn't feel like Molly. "There are days I wish I was a medium."

"Not me." She shakes her head. "I don't want that particular gift at all."

We go quiet again, but the house seems to be even quieter.

"Must have been Molly," I say at last.

Still, my instincts tell me that something is just...wrong.

And I don't know what it is.

"Hello, darling."

Mom kisses my cheek and then bolts through the door, heading straight for Breena.

"Hello, sweet girl. Oh, I'm so excited to see you!"

"I'm so glad you're home," Breena replies and opens her arms for a hug from my mom. Then, the two are off, talking a mile a minute.

"They've always gotten on well," Dad says with a smile as he comes inside so I can close the door behind him. "I think it's because they're so much alike."

"You're probably right." Dad hugs me and then claps me on the back. "I'm glad you two are home."

"Me, too. It's always good to see the family but being gone for too long makes me twitchy. How—?"

He stops cold and tips his head as if he's listening.

"What is it?"

My dad is a powerful medium and empath, and he just always *knows*.

It was a huge pain in the ass when I was a teenager.

"Interesting."

I follow his gaze up my staircase. "What?"

"Molly's telling on you." Dad laughs and then turns to me. "Congratulations."

"On what?"

"On Breena."

I shake my head and then narrow my eyes at the empty staircase. "Not cool, Molly. Not cool at all."

Dad laughs again as he follows me through the house to the back patio, where I have the grill set up and ready for some chicken.

"I think it's past time you noticed her," he says when we're out of earshot of the women.

"I've *always* noticed her."

His face registers surprise. "You didn't do anything about it."

"She's a lot younger than me, Dad. And then life took over."

"Your mother has said for years that you're meant for each other. Fated."

"Someone could have said something to *me*."

"And miss all the fun? Not on your life. Now, tell me about the work you're doing on the curse."

And so, as the chicken cooks on the grill, I fill him in on the Tapestry of Fate Breena's already started on.

"I can't believe it's been in the Book of Shadows and here in my house all this time."

"You found it when you were meant to," he insists. "I have some other grimoires and Books of Shadows from other family members in my basement. I'll take a look at them."

"Can I borrow them? It'll go faster if the six of us pore over them."

"Of course. You can pick them up anytime. I'll have them ready."

"Thanks."

"What's taking so long out here?" Mom asks as she and Breena join us outside. "We're starving."

"It's almost done."

"Breena shared her coconut cake recipe with me in exchange for my strawberry preserves recipe. I can't wait to bake that cake tomorrow. If it turns out well, I'll make another for the Beltane celebration."

"There's still so much to do to get ready for that," Breena says and nibbles her bottom lip the way she always does when she's nervous. "I feel like we'll never get everything done. And I'm in the thick of the tapestry now. Both Lucy and Lorelei have been bringing me more textiles every day, but it's such a laborious process. I don't know how I'll find the time to get ready for Beltane."

"You won't," Mom asserts happily. "I'll take over the Beltane preparations and recruit some other coven members to help. You just worry about that tapestry."

"Oh. But I couldn't do that—"

"You can," Mom assures her. "And you will. You take on too much, sweet girl. We want to help, and since I'm not one of the chosen to assist with breaking this horrible curse, I can at least take this off your plate."

Breena blinks as if she's fighting tears.

"That would be really helpful."

"You need to ask for help more often," Mom says gently. "There's no shame in it. I also have some supplies at home that might help you with the project. You're welcome to them."

"You know, adding some magic from you and your

family might be powerful," Breena agrees, thinking it over. "I think the more magic, the better."

"Then you'll have it."

Suddenly, Mom turns and stares up at a second-story window.

"Well, now that's interesting."

For the second time since they arrived, I follow one of my parent's gazes and ask, "What is?"

"It was only there for a moment," Mom replies. "Have you invited anything in, Giles?"

"Of course, not. I wouldn't do that."

"Hmm. I don't think Molly is the only spirit here."

"It's not our place to speak of it," Dad says and takes Mom's hand. "You know that."

"He's my *child*."

"What's here?" I ask, feeling my stomach roil at the idea of something or some*one* hurting Breena. "What the hell is going on?"

Mom just shakes her head and glances at me with sad eyes. "You'll be okay."

Breena and I share a nervous look.

"If I need to protect us from something—"

"You don't." Mom cups my cheek. "Not yet, anyway. Besides, you're both strong witches and have your shit together. Nothing can mess with you—especially here."

"Then why do you look so worried?"

"Because you're my child, and it's my job to worry about you."

"I don't buy it."

"Maybe I shouldn't be here," Breena says, rubbing her hand over her forehead. "If something came here because of me and ends up hurting Giles, I won't forgive myself."

"You're not going anywhere."

"But—"

"I shouldn't have said anything," Mom laments and wraps an arm around Breena's shoulders. "Nothing is your fault. Do you hear me? None of this, absolutely *none* of it is your doing, Breena. And, yes, you *should* be here. You and Giles have an important job to do together."

"But if it's not safe—"

"It is," Mom assures her, but I see the look she shares with my father, and I don't like it. Not one bit.

What aren't they saying?

"You're both stronger than you realize. And together? You're pretty much unstoppable."

"That sounds very foreboding."

"Not at all," Mom says and kisses Breena's cheek. "Now, can we please eat? I'm starving."

"It's ready." I place the chicken on a platter. When Breena takes it from me, and she and Mom walk into the house, I turn to my father. "What do I need to know?"

"Just pay attention," he urges after a long pause. "Stay alert. You'll know what to do when the time comes."

"But you won't tell me what that is?"

"It can change in the blink of an eye," he says. "You hold all the answers inside of you, Giles."

I blow out a breath and look up at the empty window.

"I need a drink. You?"

"Absolutely."

"Let's get one and join the ladies for dinner. Just promise me something."

"If I can."

I shove my hands into my pockets. "If I need to know something to keep Breena safe, you have to tell me. I can't lose her, Dad."

"If I thought her life—or yours—was in danger, I'd tell you everything you needed to know. I promise."

I nod once. "Okay. Let's go get that drink."

CHAPTER FIVE
BREENA

"I'll have more for you next week," Percy McGuire, one of the eldest members of our coven, says as he loads the last bag of wool into the back of my car. "I have more shearing to do. Then I'll have to clean the wool for you."

"I don't mind doing it," I reply and boost myself up onto my toes to kiss the man on his leathery cheek. "I just appreciate you giving me this. I wish you'd let me pay you for it, though."

"If this lifts that curse and sets those people in Hallows End free, that's all the payment I need, honey."

I take a deep breath and nod in agreement. "I know what you mean. Will any alpaca wool be ready soon?"

"I should have some in a few weeks," he says with a frown. "I could get some ready for you."

"No, not for this project," I reply, shaking my head. "For my personal use. Your alpaca wool is the best for the projects I have in mind, and I'm happy to buy it from you."

Percy smiles, and I know it's in relief. Alpaca wool is much more expensive than sheep wool.

"I'll let you know as soon as I harvest some."

"Thanks, Percy."

"Oh, Breena. The wife and I set some of our own spells on that wool while we harvested and cleaned it. Added some extra magic to it."

"I love that. The more magic, the better. Thank you."

I wave at Percy as I start my car, pull away from his little farm, and head back into town. I have one more stop to make before I can go home and continue weaving today.

After parking outside Lucy's apothecary, I walk inside and immediately smile. I love this store so much. The shelves are lined with pots and bottles full of salves, lotions, tinctures, and oils. There's a whole wall of shelves lined with gallon-sized jars full of dried herbs and plants so people can buy them in bulk for their magical workings.

And Lucy is behind the counter, crushing and mixing something with a mortar and pestle.

"Good morning," she greets with a smile as I walk over. "I'm just about ready."

"Is Lorelei here?"

"Yep, she's in the kitchen, boiling some water."

"Great, I'll go out and get the first bag of wool."

I turn to walk back outside and crash right into a hard chest.

"*I'll* get the wool," Jonas says with a kind smile as he holds my shoulders firmly, helping me regain my balance. "How are you today, Breena?"

"I'm doing well. How are you, Jonas?"

He smiles again, but I see the worry in his eyes. "I'm doing just as well. Is the car unlocked?"

"It is."

He nods and sets off to fetch the wool, and I turn to Lucy.

"He's not as well as he wants us all to believe."

She sighs and looks at the empty doorway where her husband just was. "I know. He's worried, Breena. Now that we know about the timeline to lift the curse, he gets more anxious with each day that passes, worried that we won't get it done in time."

"We will." My voice is more confident than I feel. "It's all going to be okay."

"I hope you're right. Okay, this is crushed as much as I can get it. It'll make a great purple color for the wool."

"Oh, I'm so excited." Jonas walks in carrying two bushels of wool and moves past us to the kitchen.

Lucy waves down her employee, Delia. "We'll be in the kitchen if you need anything."

"I've got this handled, boss," Delia replies with a wink. "Hi, Breena."

"Hey, you. Is that the new arnica salve?"

"Lucy just finished pouring it last night," Delia confirms.

"I'll buy one on my way out." I follow Lucy to the kitchen where Jonas has already spread one bag of wool on the table. Lorelei minds the huge stockpot on the stove.

"I never thought I'd be a woman who dyes wool by hand," she says by way of greeting. "But here we are, doing it like the olden days. Right, Jonas?"

"Well, sort of," he replies. "We didn't have an electric stove for the kettle, or—"

"I get it," Lorelei interrupts, holding up a hand. "I mean no disrespect when I say this, but I'm so glad I was born in this century."

Jonas laughs as he kisses Lucy's head. "No offense taken. I'll help Delia out front while you ladies handle this. There's not enough room back here for all of us."

"Thank you," Lucy says to him and then turns to us. "Okay, we have supplies to make red, purple, green, blue, and black."

"That's perfect. Wait, do we have yellow?"

"Yes," Lucy confirms, looking around. "Sorry. Yellow, too."

"I can work with this. I also have some gold thread coming in. With the other magical baubles everyone has promised to embellish with, I can make this a really beautiful tapestry."

"I'm so glad you know how to do this," Lorelei says. "I brought extra seaweed for the green."

"The green is important," I reply. "There will be a lot of trees in the image."

"I can always get more seaweed if we need it," she adds.

"Okay, ladies, let's get to work," Lucy says.

"This is incredible."

I glance up from the loom at the sound of Giles's voice and offer him a smile.

"It's been done this way for thousands of years. Okay, hundreds, at least." I grab another handful of green wool and begin feeding it into the loom. The teeth brush it into a soft, smooth bunch. From here, I'll feed it into a spinner to make it into yarn.

It's a whole lengthy process that has to happen before I can even start weaving the tapestry.

"This is going to take forever," I warn Giles. "Like, I hope it's finished by Samhain this fall. I know it *has* to be, but it's such a painstakingly slow process. What if I just can't do it? I have a business to run and bills to pay on top of this. Even with everyone's help, it's a lot."

"First of all, I don't want you to worry about bills, Breena."

I look up from the wool and scowl. "I'm an adult. Of course, I worry about bills."

"I've got you covered."

I smirk and begin feeding the wool again. "Right."

"I'm serious. For the foreseeable future, the only thing you need to worry about is that tapestry. You can pay me back later if it makes you feel better."

I stop again and stare up at him. "You're serious."

"I'm absolutely serious. This is a big ask of you, and we all know it. But no one else has the skill set to help, so most of this falls on your shoulders. Therefore, the five of us will handle everything else. Your bills are taken care of."

"I can't sit at this loom or the spinner twenty-four seven."

"Of course, not. But you have the freedom to work as much or as little as you want or need."

I blink and stare down at my calloused fingers, over-come with emotion. I'd never expect anyone to be responsible for me and my needs.

Yet I didn't even have to ask. They just *knew*.

"Thank you," I say at last.

"You're welcome. What can I do to help?"

I laugh and return to the task at hand. "I think you just did it."

"How about we go out for dinner?"

I raise an eyebrow and glance his way again. "Did you just ask me out on a date, Giles Corey?"

"Hell, yes, I did."

"Well, that sounds lovely. I'm going to need a break from this in about an hour or so."

"Perfect timing. I just got a new shipment of larimar

and howlite that I need to go through, so I'll be in my office."

"You don't have that shipped directly to the shop?"

"I brought it here." He shrugs when I wait for him to explain further. "I wanted to come home and see you."

"That's pretty sweet of you." He narrows his eyes, and I laugh. "Lorelei will be so excited about the larimar."

"I know. She's the reason I ordered it. It's damn expensive but necessary for a sea witch. I'll be ready to go when you are."

I nod and watch him leave the room, then rub my hand over my chest.

I was convinced that Giles wasn't for me. That no matter how much I had longed for him all these years, he wasn't fated to be mine, after all.

But now, after living here for a couple of weeks and being near him so often, after letting my guard down and letting go of the embarrassment, a light of hope fills my chest and makes me feel warm.

I sense this will be the most eventful year of my life.

"Let's walk this evening," Giles suggests as we step outside the house. "It's warm."

"It *is* a nice evening," I agree, breathing in the fresh spring air. "The trees will bloom soon."

He takes my hand and threads our fingers together, and we walk down to the sidewalk and toward town.

"What are you hungry for?" he asks.

"I don't know. What do you want?"

"Are we going to be those people? The ones who can never decide on a meal?"

"I think that's pretty much the norm, isn't it? I don't know. Are you in the mood for seafood?"

"I can always eat seafood. Let's do that."

I nod and then settle into the quiet of the early evening as we walk side by side to our favorite waterfront restaurant.

"I think Xander's been at sea for about a week," I say as the ships come into view. "It always makes me nervous."

"That's understandable. Your dad and both of your uncles were killed on a fishing boat."

I nod thoughtfully. "I wonder if that's one of the reasons Lorelei resists what's between her and Xander. Maybe she's afraid of losing him the way her mom lost her dad."

"That could be," Giles says slowly. "At least, it could be a factor. But I think it goes much deeper than that."

"I do, too. Something happened between them. Something that made her leave town for two *years*. But she won't tell us what it was. She won't give us any details at all, and that's incredibly frustrating because we tell each other everything."

"Maybe she thinks she's protecting you from something," he suggests. "Or maybe it's because Xander is the leader of our coven. Perhaps she doesn't want to make the two of you dislike him and make it hard for you to work with him."

"It really could be any of those things," I admit. "It's just frustrating because whenever we ask, she changes the subject. She's so dang stubborn."

"And smart." He leads me to the door of the restaurant and holds it open for me. "Table for two, please."

The hostess consults a board on her podium and then gestures for us to follow her.

I love Salem. I love the diversity here, and all the different people who live here and come to visit. Some are eclectic with piercings and loud hair colors. Others are more subdued. But for the most part, they're all friendly and happy to be here.

We wind our way through tables to a booth in the back against the windows with a beautiful view of the water.

"Well, this is lovely."

I accept the menu and then smile over at Giles, who watches me through his glasses, his expression serious.

"You look wonderful this evening," he says when the hostess leaves.

"Thanks. After finishing at the loom, I was a bit of a mess."

"No, you're pretty much always hot as hell." He casually sips his water as if he just made a comment about his favorite football team and didn't just knock me off my axis. "What's your favorite thing to get here?"

"I usually go for the fresh sea bass," I reply, feeling my stomach growl. "In fact, that sounds really good. How about you?"

"This close to Maine? Lobster, of course."

"Ooh, let's get both and share."

"You're on."

Suddenly, I feel the hair on the back of my neck stand on end as if someone's watching me. I glance around the restaurant but don't see anyone looking our way.

"What's wrong?" Giles asks.

"I just had a weird feeling. I'm sure it's nothing."

He reaches out and takes my hand. "I don't believe in coincidences these days. What was the feeling?"

"It just seemed like we were being watched." I shrug a shoulder and reach for my water. "But I'm sure it's nothing, Giles. There's just a lot of energy in this room."

His eyes narrow, and then he glances around but doesn't say anything before the waitress arrives to take our order.

Dinner passes quickly, full of excellent food and even better conversation. Before long, we're walking home with full bellies.

"That was *amazing*," I say with a sigh as we approach the house. "The food and the company. Thanks."

"You're welcome."

He follows me up the steps to the front door but doesn't unlock it.

"I'm going to kiss you out here on the porch, the way it should be after a date."

I grin up at him. "You won't hear me complain."

He leans in, brushes his fingertips down my cheek, and lays his lips on mine, gently at first, and then he deepens the kiss.

My back is suddenly pressed to the door, and I let my purse fall to the porch as I loop my arms around his neck.

My goddess, I want to climb him. I want to strip out of my dress and let him have his way with me. I want *everything* with this man.

When he groans into my neck, nibbling his way up to my ear, I know he feels exactly the same way.

"You're so fucking amazing." The whisper is rough and full of need, but before I can respond, I hear a very distinct *meow.*

Giles lifts his head and stares down at me.

"Do you have a cat?" I ask him.

"No. I'm allergic." He backs away, far enough for us to look down. Sure enough, a cat sits, staring up at us.

"You're a witch, and you're allergic to *cats*?"

"Yeah. Ironic, I know." He looks down at the feline. "You're lost, buddy."

"He's not lost."

Giles's gaze turns back to me. "What? I didn't know you had a cat."

"I haven't in a while," I confess, still looking at the black cat staring right at me. "But I'm sure that's Merlin. My familiar."

Giles sighs. "I'll call the doctor and get my allergy meds refilled."

"Hold on." I squat and reach out. The cat rests his chin in my hand, the same way Merlin used to do. "Hey there, baby. This is a surprise and not the best timing, but I'm so glad to see you. Did you just know I needed you?"

Meow. His green eyes narrow as he walks over to bump his head against mine. *Meow.*

"I'll keep him in my bedroom," I offer, but Giles is already shaking his head.

"I'll be fine with some medicine," he says. "It's not *that* bad. How did you know so quickly that it was him?"

"Because I *know*. A witch recognizes her familiar. He's been gone for three years."

"Like, he ran off?"

"No, he died of old age."

"Familiars reincarnate?"

"Of course, they do."

He shakes his head, looks at the cat, and then unlocks the door. "You learn something new every day."

"Didn't your parents have familiars?"

"No, we're all allergic."

"Well, I'm sorry for that, because having Merlin with me is the most comforting and *helpful* thing I've ever had in my practice."

"I wonder how he found you."

I simply smile at Giles as I lift the cat and kiss his cheek. "He's mine, and I'm his. It was inevitable he'd find his way to me."

"He looks well cared for. No fleas or anything."

I look down at the cat and smile. "No, you've been loved, haven't you?"

"Maybe someone's looking for him."

Meow.

"I don't think so. Are you sure this is okay?"

Giles shrugs. "It seems there's not much I *won't* do for you, Breena. It's just fine."

Chapter Six

His strength grows, rejuvenating him much faster than ever before. It fills him with satisfaction and anticipation. He was able to leave Hallows End without a host, which is a handicap, but something he can deal with.

He's not confined.

He can hunt.

And his prey is already in sight.

They thought they could beat him. Outsmart him. But he's been hunting for centuries.

They're nothing.

And he will remind them very soon just how insignificant they are.

Chapter Seven
Giles

"Give me. Right now." Lorelei comes marching into my shop like a woman on a mission, her dark auburn hair a riot of curls around her beautiful face. She plants her hands on my countertop and leans toward me. "Larimar. I want it."

I grin at her and shove my glasses up my nose. "You must have talked with Breena."

"Of course, I did. I talk to her every day. And she spilled the tea about some new larimar in the shop. I need it."

"Well, you were the witch I had in mind when I bought it." I wipe my hands and walk around to the glass case where I store the most precious crystals. "I have several sizes."

I spread everything out for her and watch her pupils dilate in excitement. I understand. It's a stunning crystal, mined only in the ocean off the Dominican Republic.

It's not easy to get, given its volcanic origins, and it's damn expensive.

But it also looks like the ocean, with its turquoise-blue color rippled with white, giving it the look of the Caribbean.

"I want it all."

My eyes whip up to hers. "Lora, there's about a thousand dollars-worth here. And that's *my* cost."

"I want it," she insists, shaking her head. "You even have little chips here that I can use in candle work. The quality is amazing. It's definitely not fake."

I feel my hackles rise and narrow my eyes at her. "You won't find man-made crystals in my shop at any time."

Her face softens into a smile. "Sorry, I wasn't implying otherwise. It's just...this is so hard to find, and I'm excited. I'm not kidding, Giles, I want it all."

"You're the customer." I start wrapping it for her. "How are things with you? Are you settled into the cottage?"

"I am. I have it all set up the way I want, and my office faces the water so I can draw energy from the ocean while I write. I walk the shoreline several times a day."

"See any mermaids?" I ask. It was always a joke when we were younger that Lorelei could talk to all the under-water creatures, even the mermaids.

"Daily. They're real, you know."

"So you say."

"For a witch, you're awfully cynical."

I laugh and bag up her order. When I tell her the total, she scowls.

"I know it's more than that."

"My cost." I shrug when she just stares at me. "It's expensive enough as it is. Don't worry about it. I mean it."

"I see what Breena sees in you," she says as I run her credit card. "You're just a nice guy."

"Don't let it get out. Is there anything else you'd like me to keep an eye out for?"

"Nothing specific, but I'll let you know if I think of anything. Thanks for this. I have an altar to fiddle with, candles to make, and that huge piece is going on my mantel."

"Have fun with it."

Lorelei heads out of the shop with a happy wave, and I decide to step outside and get some fresh air. I've been at work since early this morning. I couldn't sleep after a particularly nasty nightmare and figured I'd just come in.

The bad dreams have gotten worse since Breena moved into the house. I feel like something is ramping up again, but we have close to six months before Samhain and the next round with the witch killer.

This is the supposed *downtime* when we can research, plan, and feel safe.

But something tells me we need to keep our guards up.

So, I came to work early this morning so I could close early and get home to Breena.

One thing is for sure, the weather this spring has been unseasonably warm. After a harsh winter, the sunshine is welcome.

But as I step outside, everything goes dark. There's no light at all, and as I reach behind me for Gems' door, I find that's gone, too.

"Hello?"

My voice echoes as if I'm in a tunnel. I can hear water dripping, and something flutters by my face, making me jerk back. I slam into a brick wall.

One that wasn't there mere seconds ago.

"You have no power here!" I yell as the wind starts to pick up. I root my feet and feel the power of the earth beneath me as I raise my hands into the air and begin chanting a protection spell.

"Evil spirits that roam this place, be thee gone from time and space. From rise of moon to set of sun, I banish your essence, your power is none. My word is my will, my steadfast decree. All this I say, so mote it be."

Snow and ice fall, pelting my face as the temperature drops, and the wind swirls around me. But I don't waver in the spell or my stance.

Finally, everything just...stops. Suddenly, I'm standing out in the sunshine on a pretty spring day in Salem.

People walk past on Essex Street, not even giving me a second glance, as if I hadn't been screaming a protection and banishing spell into the wind moments ago.

Everything is just...normal.

But when I turn to walk back inside, my shop is gone, and I'm standing in front of a house on an uneven, cobblestone street.

A noise behind me has me turning in surprise, and I see that all of modern Essex Street is gone. There are buildings, small ones I know from history lessons are a church, a brothel, and several homes.

And there's so much water. Four hundred years ago, the waterfront almost came up to Essex Street.

Horses and people on foot hurry past, paying me no mind. It's as though I'm invisible to them.

A mob of people hover in a circle, and I walk over to see what they're looking at.

"Just confess." A man in his twenties—maybe thirties—stands over an older man lying on the ground, a door on top of him and a pile of boulders on the slab of wood.

He's being pressed to death.

"Giles Corey, you must either confess or plead not guilty."

"I will not," Giles says and then groans when they roll another boulder onto the door.

For the love of all the gods, I'm witnessing the torture and execution of Giles Corey.

"Confess, witch!" the crowd chants. Some cry in pity. Others cheer.

It's complete pandemonium.

And when I look to my right, I see Jonas standing

back in the crowd, watching Giles, his face set in hard lines.

His gaze moves to me, and he *sees* me.

Does he recognize me?

"Jonas!"

His eyes narrow, and he turns to walk away, quickly making his way through the crowd.

When I try to hurry after him, I'm swallowed by the pandemonium of the bloodthirsty crowd, demanding my death.

No, not mine.

Giles from 1692.

"Giles?" Someone taps my shoulder, and I whip around, ready to fight.

"What?"

"Hey." Xander steps back, his hands raised in surrender. "Are you okay?"

I spin around and see that everything is as it should be. No public execution. Modern buildings.

But my heart continues pounding in my chest, and my mouth is dry when I turn back to Xander, who's studying me with narrowed, black eyes.

"Yeah. Yeah, I'm okay."

"Let's go inside, shall we?"

"Right." I nod and lead the way back to my shop. After pushing my way inside, Xander walks in behind me and locks the door.

"Tell me what happened."

I sigh and lick my lips, then shove my hand through my hair. "I think I was hallucinating."

I describe everything I saw.

"Jonas was there?" he asks.

"Yes, and he saw me. No one else noticed me, like I was a ghost, but he saw me. And when I called out his name, he ran."

"Fascinating," Xander mutters as he paces my shop.

"Something wanted to scare me today."

He turns to me. "And from the look of you, it succeeded."

"Hell, yeah, it did. It was fucking terrifying." I pace in agitation. "Fuck, I need to call Breena and make sure she's safe."

I reach for my phone and tap the screen to call her.

"Hello?"

The sound of her sweet voice almost sends me to my knees.

"Are you okay?"

"Uh, yeah. I'm just working at the loom. Why wouldn't I be okay? Are *you* okay?"

I blow out a breath, and my knees want to give out in relief. "I'm not okay, but I will be. I'll tell you about it when I get home. I'm headed that way in just a few minutes."

"So early?"

"I'll close for the day. I'll see you soon. And, Breena, I want you to stay put and keep Merlin with you until I get there."

"You're scaring me."

"Just stay put."

I hang up and turn to Xander, who smiles at me.

"What?"

"You two are figuring it out."

"We're trying, but it's a little hard with a curse and a murderer hanging over our heads, Xander."

He nods and blows out a breath. "Yeah, I can see that. I don't think you were truly in danger today. I suspect it was just a scare tactic."

"I don't like it."

"I don't either. I think the six of us should get together and talk with Jonas. And we need to refresh the wards and cast some protection spells."

"It's too soon."

Xander and I just look at each other for several seconds, both of us grim with worry.

"I know," he agrees at last. "I thought we'd have the full year."

"We don't. I know we don't."

A door in the apartment above slams shut, surprising me.

"I don't have spirits here. What the fuck?"

He turns and seems to watch something in the corner of the room.

"You need to go," he says, his voice deep with authority as he claps his hands loudly three times. "You're not welcome here."

He watches for a moment and then nods.

"It's gone."

"What was it?"

"Energy. There's a lot of energy around town right now, and I don't like it. I felt it as soon as I got off the boat this morning."

"Beltane is two weeks away."

"I don't think we can wait two weeks to speak with the coven." His mouth is set in grim lines. "Let's talk with the others first and then bring in the rest of the group."

"You're all welcome to come to my place tonight."

Xander nods. "Let's make it happen. I'll see you then. I'm going to escort you home, Giles. I don't think you should be alone."

"You know, ordinarily I'd tell you I'm fine, and it's not a big deal. But today, I'm going to take you up on that offer."

"I wasn't there when Giles was pressed to death," Jonas says, shaking his head. "At that point, I hadn't figured out that I could move between worlds yet. I didn't know for some time that he'd been killed."

"So it wouldn't have been possible for me to see you in that crowd?"

Jonas shakes his head. "No. If you were witnessing an actual historical moment, I wouldn't have been there."

"It wasn't time travel. It was a bunch of bullshit," Lorelei spits, her eyes firing with anger. "It was a vision designed to scare you."

"It worked," I mutter and rub my hand over my mouth. "I can honestly say that if I never see a man tortured like that again, it will be too soon. You hear about it, you even see reenactments of it, but let me tell you, it's far worse than you can even imagine."

"What's it saying?" Breena wonders. "Is it warning you that it's going to try to do that to you, too? That you'll meet the same fate?"

"Have you seen all the witches in Salem? We don't persecute people for that anymore," Lucy says, but I shake my head.

"You might be on to something. What if this is the...*thing* that tried to kill Breena? That killed Agatha?"

"But it can't come back until Samhain," Lorelei assures, shaking her head emphatically.

"Can't it?" I demand. "Why not? It failed last time, and that changed everything. What if it *can* come back now because it failed?"

"I don't have the energy to fight a homicidal paranormal entity more than once a year," Lucy says as she hangs her head in her hands. "Seriously, this is getting out of hand."

"*Getting* out of hand?" Breena asks.

"We need to rally the troops," Xander decides. "We're all back on high alert for the foreseeable future. That means I won't be out at sea for a while either."

Lorelei's shoulders sag in relief. I share a look with Breena, but neither of us says anything.

"I'm about to start spinning the wool into yarn," Breena says. "Nothing about this Tapestry of Fate will be quick. It's a long process, and I was worried about making it in time for Samhain as it was. Now, I have to worry about having it done faster?"

"No one is pressuring you," Xander assures her. "It'll get done when it's done. In the meantime, we need to reinforce the protections and work together to keep one another safe."

"I feel like we should move into a communal house so we can protect each other," Lucy mutters.

"I don't want to listen to all of you having sex," Lorelei says with a sigh. "No thanks. I'm perfectly safe in the cottage by the sea."

"I don't want you to hex me for saying this or anything, but maybe Xander should stay with you, Lorelei."

She snorts and shakes her head. "Absolutely not. Never in this or any other lifetime. You'd have to kill me first."

"Something tells me she doesn't like that idea," Breena says.

"None of us likes the thought of you being alone," Lucy states, trying to be reasonable. "You've said yourself that there is safety in numbers."

"I'm *fine*," Lorelei insists. "Now, let's change the subject before I get really mad."

"So stubborn," Breena mutters. "Fine. But if things ramp up and get really dangerous, you'll move in here, and you won't argue with me."

"Since when did you get bossy?" Lorelei wants to know.

"When a maniac killed me." Breena swallows hard. "He won't get the chance to hurt any of you. Absolutely not."

"I need to make sure that Hallows End is safe, as well," Jonas adds. "So far, everything there is normal—as it can be. But we may need to intervene if things start deviating from that norm the way they did last fall."

"Agreed," Xander says with a nod. "Let's get to work."

Chapter Eight
Breena

"Hello, pumpkin."

I smile at my mom and then laugh a little at the term of endearment. It's always seemed like such a silly nickname to me.

"Hi, Mom. What are you doing?"

"Why, I'm just working on my journal." I notice she's writing in a big book, using an old-fashioned quill and ink. The feather is that of a peacock, and it's beautiful.

"I've never seen that quill before."

"Oh, it's an old one. It was your great-grandmother's. I only use it when I have something important to write down."

She smiles at me again, but this time it's not the typical loving grin my mother usually gives me.

No, it's hard. Sinister.

"Mom?"

"You know, I didn't think it was such a good idea in

the beginning, but the more I thought about it, the more I liked it."

"What idea, Mom?"

She blinks up at me as if she's been in a haze.

"What? Oh, hello, pumpkin."

"You were telling me about an idea."

That sinister smile slips over her lips once more. "We're not really supposed to talk about it, but it's such a good idea."

"What is it?"

"How we're going to kill you three girls, of course."

I back away and knock over a bookshelf, sending hard-covers skittering across the hardwood floor.

"What?"

"Now, don't act like that. It wouldn't be so hard if you hadn't had the wards tattooed on the backs of your necks. But I think we're finding a way around those."

"You're not my mom."

Just like that, the form changes from my mother to the man who held me hostage in my house on Samhain.

The one from Hallows End who tried to kill me.

But it wasn't the man himself who'd attempted to murder me. Something evil had possessed him.

"Hello."

His voice is a hiss like a snake, and it makes my skin crawl.

"You're not real."

He's walking, circling me, and we're in the dark,

somehow in the middle of a spotlight. I don't know where we are.

When I try to turn and run, my feet won't move.

"You can't leave," he hisses and moves closer to me. His face is mere inches from mine, and he drops that jaw in a horrible, awkward way that looks as if his jaw is unhinged. And then he screams.

"Oh, goddess."

I jump out of bed, my heart racing and breath coming fast, and hurry to turn on the lights. Merlin was sleeping on the bed, but he lifts his head and blinks his green eyes at me.

"Holy shit," I mutter, grasping my hands between my breasts and trying to catch my breath.

"Hey." Giles hurries into my room, topless and bathed in sweat. Then, without a word, he yanks me to him, wraps his arms around me, and holds me tightly. "Are you okay?"

"Nightmare," I mutter against his bare, muscled chest.

"Me, too, but I woke up to you screaming."

I frown and pull back to look up at him. "I screamed?"

"Oh, yeah. I'm pretty sure they heard you down in Boston."

Having him here like this is comforting, and I'm beginning to settle just a bit. When he leads me back to the bed, I don't argue. We sit, our backs against the headboard, and he pulls me against him again as if he *has* to have me in his arms, to make sure I'm safe. His skin is warm and smooth, and resting my cheek against his chest feels good.

"Wanna talk about it?" I ask.

"I couldn't get to you." I hear him swallow thickly. "You were crying out, and *it* was taunting you, and I was on the outside again, unable to protect you."

I tighten my grip on him. "That sounds pretty horrible. I'm sorry."

"What about yours?"

"I think it was the same dream, except from the other perspective. He had me, I couldn't run, and he was taunting me."

He buries his lips in my hair, and we sit quietly for a moment, simply holding on to each other.

"I'm sorry, too," he says at last.

"It's not your fault." I look up at him and cup his rough cheek in my hand. "None of this is any fault of ours. What I don't like is that he used my mom to hurt me in this one, and she would *never* hurt me."

"No, she wouldn't." He kisses my head again. "Let's at least try to get some sleep."

"Okay." I'm not quite ready for him to go, but he's right; we need all the rest we can get these days. "Thanks for coming to check on me. I'll see you tomorrow."

But he doesn't move. When I look into his eyes, I see they're full of humor.

"What?" I ask.

"I'd like to stay here. As in, *we* should try to get some sleep."

"Oh, I probably won't have another nightmare. You don't have to stay just to take care of me."

"No, I'd like to stay so you can protect *me* from the nightmares. You'll be doing me a favor, Breena."

I can't help but laugh a little as I scoot down so I can lie on the queen-sized bed.

"Merlin sleeps on the bed, and you're allergic."

"I got the medicine. I'll be fine."

Giles cuts the light and lies down, facing me in the moonlight.

"Will it always be like this?" I ask in a whisper.

"What do you mean?"

"Scary. Uncertain. Mostly just scary."

"No, sweetheart." He cups my cheek, and I can see the concern in his eyes, even in the dim light. "It won't be. We'll get through this, and life can get back to normal, whatever that means."

"I know our normal isn't normal at all to some people. But I miss it, and I can't wait to have it back."

"I'm with you there." He kisses my forehead. "Sleep. We can deal with everything in the morning."

I'm surprised to find that I actually feel sleepy, and with his arm loosely draped around my waist, I let myself fall into a dreamless slumber.

Giles was gone when I woke up this morning.

And, yeah, a part of me was disappointed. Giles has been incredibly affectionate with me since our date. He's sweet, but he hasn't made any advances in the sex direction, and I'm just too inexperienced to make the moves on him.

I wouldn't know where to start.

Not to mention, is it weird to have sex on the brain when we're trying to combat something evil and solve a curse?

Maybe.

"I'm not going to worry about it," I say to Merlin, who's sitting on my altar, watching me shuffle my tarot cards. I should be at the spinner, turning the wool into yarn, but after that particularly nasty nightmare last night, I felt I needed to spend some time grounding and talking with my spirit guides and ancestors.

I've already lit the candles, so I close my eyes and take some deep breaths as I continue to shuffle.

"Good morning," I begin, speaking out loud to the spirits with me. "I'd like to spend some time with my guides and ancestors, both known and unknown. Those who support my highest good. I need some advice and guidance as I navigate this difficult time."

I take another deep breath, set the deck on my altar, cut it into three piles, and get to work.

I always have a notebook and pen nearby when I work with tarot so I can jot down notes in case what I pull doesn't make sense in the moment but will later when I look back.

For an hour, I ask questions and pull cards, making my notes. Some messages confuse me, so I pull out my pendulum and start asking yes or no questions for clarity.

It might be the most intense session I've ever had with my guides. I've never needed to go this deep before.

But goddess knows I need all the help I can get right now. I've never felt so uncertain or *scared*. It's unsettling, to say the least, and I want to feel empowered.

"Thank you," I say at last, taking another deep breath. "When I blow out this candle, the session is closed, and I ask that no spirits stay."

I snuff out the candle and then look over at Merlin, who's been watching me steadily the whole time.

"Some odd messages came through, but also some that made total sense. I'll make some more notes and think it all over."

"Meow."

"You've always enjoyed altar work." I lean in to brush my nose against his. "I'm so happy you're here. You were gone a long while this time."

"Meow."

I grin and kiss his head. Lucy has a familiar, a huge Irish Wolfhound named Nera, and they can communicate telepathically. I've never been able to do that with Merlin. In fact, I don't have any telepathic or clairvoyant gifts at all. It can be annoying sometimes, but I think it's for the best.

I'm an empath and tend to take on the emotions of those around me. If I could *hear* their feelings and thoughts, it might unsettle me.

I bustle into the kitchen and check the protection pot simmering on the stove. I've been letting it go all day, feeling the need to add the extra layer of protection to the house.

"Well, that's about done, isn't it?" Turning off the stove, I set the pot aside to cool. Everything I used is organic and can be returned to the earth later.

My phone pings with a text, and I grin when I see Giles's name on the readout.

Giles: *We're meeting with the coven in an hour. Want me to pick you up on the way?*

I tap out my response to accept the offer and then sigh.

"I'm not going to get as much done today as I'd hoped." Merlin blinks up at me. "Come on, we can at least get the yarn we've made so far organized by color. You know, I'm going to have to start sketching out what this tapestry should look like. Should it be Hallows End *before* the curse was cast? And if that's the case, will all those people age and die in a matter of moments? Will the same happen to Jonas? I'll have to ask the others what they think of the design. I also have about a dozen orders that came in this week that I need to get out the door."

Merlin continues to listen silently.

"I wish you had opposable thumbs so you could help me."

"Meow."

"Yeah, yeah, I know. Okay, let's get this organized for later. You can't go with me today."

Suddenly, Merlin's back arches, and he bares his teeth, hissing.

"What in the world?"

I turn and look up to where he's staring, up the staircase.

"There's nothing there."

I don't think there's anything there.

"Molly? Is that you?"

A door slams upstairs, and Merlin cowers between my legs.

"That's just Molly. I'm sorry, sweetie, I should have introduced you." I pluck up the cat and nuzzle his black face. "Molly, this is Merlin. He's my familiar, and he'll be staying here with me for a while. Please don't frighten him. He's no threat to you."

The door slams once more, and then the lights above the staircase, that I currently have turned *off*, flicker.

"Maybe she's not a cat person," I mutter with a scowl as Merlin growls low in his throat. "Okay, you can go with me today, but you'll have to be in the carrier."

Something tells me he won't mind that. I can feel that he's frightened, and I don't like that at all.

"No need to be a jerk, Molly," I say loudly enough for the ghost to hear. "He's just a cat. You need to work on your mood."

Grateful that I already thought to buy Merlin a new

carrier because I would need to take him to the vet soon, I pull it out of a closet and set it by the door, ready for when Giles picks us up.

"Come on, sweetie. Let's go get some chores done before it's time to go."

———

"You found Merlin," Lucy says with surprise when she sees me carrying the cat in his little carrier. Nera is at her side and leans in to give Merlin a sniff. The cat just purrs at him as if having a little familiar conversation. "Oh, Breena, I'm so happy for you."

"Me, too." I hold him up so Lucy and Lorelei can look in at him. "Molly, the house ghost, wasn't being very nice to him earlier, so I brought him with me."

"Spirits always like to taunt the animals." Lorelei smiles. "Aww, he's so sweet. He even has the same little white mark on the tip of his ear."

"I know. I wasn't expecting him to look pretty much *exactly* the same."

"Oh." Lorelei's eyes widen, and she squats to be at eye level with Merlin. "Is that right?"

"What did he tell you?" I ask.

"Just that you're struggling a bit, and he's worried about you." Lorelei stands and narrows her eyes at me. "We're all worried about you."

"Giles helped." I shrug and look down when both Lucy's and Lorelei's eyebrows rise. "Not like *that*."

"And why *not* like that?" Lucy wants to know, but before I can answer, a raven lands on a low limb in the courtyard behind the aunts' house, and Lorelei makes a point to walk in the opposite direction.

Before our eyes, Xander shifts from the raven into himself, shoves his hands into his pockets, and scowls at my cousin's back.

Lucy and I share a look. "So, nothing's changed there," I say softly, and Lucy shakes her head.

It's so pretty back here in the courtyard that we have our coven meetings here when the weather allows. My mom comes outside carrying a tray of orange and rosemary cookies—my favorite—and when she sets them on a table, I hurry over to give her a big hug.

"Well, hello to you, too." She laughs. But when she pulls back and sees my face, her smile falls. "What's wrong?"

"Just a bad dream." I hold her hands reassuringly. "I'm okay, but it's really good to see you."

"Oh, sweet girl, it's always good to see you."

"Do you have a peacock writing quill?" I ask, remembering the nightmare.

She shakes her head. "No, I don't."

"I didn't think so."

Lorelei's mom, Aunt Astrid, bustles out the back door, wiping her hands on her apron.

"Hello, everyone." She smiles in welcome. "Hilda

and I made cookies, and there are plenty more inside, so help yourselves."

"You make the best cookies," Giles says as he grabs one and takes a bite. "Oh, yeah. Good stuff."

"Your mother is here, you know," his mom deadpans.

"Sorry, Ma." But Giles just grins and eats another cookie.

"I'd like to get started right away," I say to Xander, who raises an eyebrow at the request. "I'm sorry, I don't mean to overstep—"

"Not at all," Xander assures me, shaking his head. "It was just unexpected."

"I don't want to lose the whole workday," I confess and bite my lip. "I have so much to do."

"Then let's jump in," Mom suggests as we all take seats in a circle, some of us in chairs and others on the grass. Some witches prefer to sit on the ground and feel the Earth's energy radiating through them.

Lucy is one of those. Nera lies beside her.

"First, I think we should update everyone on what's been going on," Xander says and looks over at Jonas and then Giles. "You should tell your story first."

And so, for the next half hour or so, we fill the others in on all that's happened. Everything from supposed time slips to nightmares.

"It's escalating," Mr. Corey guesses. "I've felt the energy shifting in Salem since we got home from Philly."

"I've sensed the same thing," Lorelei admits. "And

that was before I knew about what happened with Giles. *Something's* in town."

"How fresh are the protection wards on your homes and businesses?" Astrid asks.

"I cast new spells every day," I answer. "I keep a simmer pot on the stove, carry black tourmaline, and scatter fresh salt in all four corners, every single day."

"Good, those are all good," Xander says with a nod. "But we can do more. We know that despite all our protection spells and wards, the bastard was able to get to us anyway. We need to do more this time."

"There's been no change in Hallows End," Jonas offers, looking around the group. "Everything is as it should be there."

"That's a good sign," Xander replies. "Mr. Corey was nice enough to loan us some old grimoires he had stored away so we can continue our research. If anyone here has anything like that they're willing to loan us, I'd really appreciate it."

"I think you need more people doing that research with you," Percy adds. "That's a lot of information for the six of you to comb through."

"Five," I counter, shaking my head. "All my time is focused on the Tapestry of Fate. And I have questions on that, too."

"Well, it seems we have our work cut out for us today," Mom says and pulls a notebook out of her apron and then plucks a pencil out of her hair, which never fails to make me smile. "Let's start with some lists and go from there."

It takes all day and breaking off into teams so we can cover ground quicker.

My mom, Giles, and Jonas, along with some of the more artistic members of the coven, join me in figuring out the tapestry.

"What if it's not a scene from Hallows End *before* the curse," Mom says slowly, "but rather of a celebration in Hallows End once the curse is lifted? Perhaps we infuse our magic into simply making it happen. Manifestation."

"I think you're on to something there," Jonas chimes in, excitement in his eyes. "If it's a celebration happening in the modern-day world, we won't have to worry about the aging and passing of the townspeople."

"Oh, I like that a *lot*." I nod vigorously. "I was worried about that the most."

"You're not the only one," Jonas replies and pats my shoulder.

"So, a modern-day celebration," I mutter, making notes. "I wish I could see it. The village, that is. I've never been there, so I don't know how to translate what it looks like into the design."

"I wonder if Jonas can take you," Xander says, clearly overhearing our conversation.

"It's worth a try." I'm excited as I turn to Jonas, but he looks apprehensive. "What? Lucy's been there."

"Because she's my soulmate," he replies. "And it was

risky. If you go with me, no one in the village can see you. It could be catastrophic."

"Okay, I'll go first thing in the morning when it's light enough for me to see, but not many people are out and about."

"It's a village stuck in time, more than three hundred years ago," Jonas reminds me. "These people tend to live-stock. They're up very early."

"Okay, what about evening before it gets dark? That should be dinnertime, right?"

"That might work," Jonas mutters.

"I have to go during the day. I won't be able to see anything in the dark."

"I wish he could just smuggle in a camera," Mom says.

"I'd really like to see it for myself," I reply and reach over to rub her back in reassuring strokes. "Please, Jonas, let's try."

"Okay. Let me think about what day is best."

"Oh, this is exciting." I clap my hands, but when I glance over at Xander, I see the worry in his eyes. "What is it?"

"Nothing." He shakes his head. "Nothing at all."

CHAPTER NINE
GILES

"Oh, what a cute little rock shop."

I look up and offer the customers a smile. The warm weather brings more and more tourists to Salem, leaving the off-season in the past. I'd welcome the additional business at any other time, but my mind is currently occupied with thoughts of Breena at home alone and all the work we have to do.

Still, I have a business to run.

"Not just rocks," the other says, pointing my way. "It looks like they have *real* jewelry, too."

"Wow, okay."

I wave at the two women. "Hello. Welcome. Is there anything in particular I can help you find?"

"Well, we're sort of new witches. Baby witches," customer number one reveals with a nervous smile. "And I *love* crystals and stuff."

"Oh, me, too," woman number two agrees with a

vigorous head bob, sending her blue and pink hair waving around her face.

"You've come to the right place," I assure them. "I have a pretty vast crystal collection here, and you're welcome to browse. If you want to see anything in the cases, let me know."

"Do you have crystals shaped like moons?" Number Two asks.

"I have a few, actually." I walk over to the other side of the room and point out amethyst, carnelian, and rose quartz, all in moon shapes. I can't help but smile as the ladies ooh and ahh over them all.

"I definitely have to get the amethyst," Number One says. "And look, there's one shaped like a wolf howling at the moon."

"That's obsidian," I inform her. "It's excellent for protection."

"I think I might spend most of my souvenir money in here," Number Two replies. "But I *have* to save enough to build my own broom later today."

"Yes," I inform her. "You do. It's a lot of fun and an important tool for a witch."

Her eyes go wide. "Are *you* a witch?"

Oh, young one, if you only knew.

"Yes," I reply simply. "If you'd like, I can help you choose some crystals that every witch should have in her toolbox, ones that won't break the debit card. You should still be able to build your brooms and buy a witch's hat at one of the other shops, as well."

"Those hats are cute," Number One whispers. "I'm in."

"Me, too," the other says.

"Okay, what do you already have at home?"

For a long while, the girls fill me in on what they already own, and I help them plug some gaps. I smile when we're standing at the counter with their loot spread out before us.

"This is a *very* nice collection for both of you. These crystals will be with you in your practice for a very long time. I'm going to gift you each a selenite bowl so you can cleanse them in it periodically."

"We have to cleanse them?" Number One asks.

"Yes. Crystals hang on to energy. Sometimes, that's good. Other times, it's not so good. Personally, I like to cleanse and charge my stones under a full moon. That's as simple as setting them on a windowsill exposed to the moonlight. But don't worry, even if you can't see the moon, if it's full, it's still powerful. Between the full moons, I set my crystals on the selenite."

"How do you cleanse the selenite?" Number Two asks.

"Good question. You're both going to be very good at your craft. Selenite is self-cleansing. It doesn't have to be charged or cleaned. And you shouldn't do much more than dust it from environmental things because selenite is water soluble and will melt. I'm also going to give you some selenite sticks. I recommend placing them above a major doorway so you cleanse the energy on the way in and out of your home."

"You're so smart," Number One says. "You should give classes on this."

"I have an advantage. I was born a witch and come from a long, long line of the same. You'll catch on; you just have to study. There are many books you can read, and I'll give you directions to the best bookstore in town. The ladies there can help you out."

"Thank you *so much*," Number Two gushes. "I could hug you. Also, you're, like, really hot."

I blink at her and then laugh. "Well, thanks."

"She's right. Are you married or anything? 'Cause maybe we could do dinner or something."

And here I thought Breena might be too young for me. I could be these girls' father.

"I'm flattered, but I am, indeed, taken."

"The good ones always are," Number One says with a sorrowful sigh.

I tally up each of their orders, and they both stare at me in shock.

"That's *it*?" Number Two demands. "But I pay way more than that online."

"You need to be careful about who you buy from," I inform them. "There are scammers out there who over-charge because crystals are becoming trendy again, and the customer doesn't know any better. Not to mention, you should always buy from dealers who ethically source their stock."

"Do you sell online?" Number One asks.

"Sorry, no. I'm a one-person show here, and I don't have time. But that could change in the future."

Maybe I could get Breena to help me with an online store of some kind. I'd have to ask her.

"I'll take your card," Number Two says. "Just in case."

"I appreciate it." I wrap and bag up their crystals, then pass the packages over once they've paid. "Have a lot of fun in Salem, ladies. It's a special place."

"I know," Number One agrees with excitement. "Do you know that a guy was *stoned* to death here? I don't think that's nearly as fun as it sounds."

I blink at her.

"You know? *Stoned*. Like, with weed."

Number Two nudges her friend. "Weed doesn't kill, you moron. Come on, we have to make our brooms."

"Have fun." I wave them off and blow out a breath after the door closes behind them.

I enjoy the tourists and helping them choose the stones that are just right for them and their needs. It's why I opened the shop. Surprisingly, I do as well with the fine jewelry as I do with the crystals.

It's a great balance for me.

But there are moments when a customer seems to just suck the energy from me.

So, I pick up my personal selenite wand and walk around the space, cleansing it of any residual energy.

Suddenly, I hear a crash behind me. I spin to find a

shelf on the wall has collapsed, the crystals from it falling onto the counter below, and some of the stones broken in two.

"Well, shit."

Before I can walk over to inspect the damage, one of the geodes levitates and launches right at me.

I dive out of the way, and the stone hits the wall behind me.

"Stop!" I order, my voice strong and loud, and then I go right into a protection spell.

"Shield this body, protect this place, redirect darkness through time and space. What's been sent will reflect on thee, not just equal but three times three. Love and light surround us all, from coyote's howl to raven's call. Guides, ancestors, deities, friends, lend me your strength without end."

All the activity stops immediately, but something pulls my attention to the large piece of labradorite that's been handed down through my family, and I narrow my eyes.

If something decides to act up while I'm gone, I don't need it to damage that piece.

"I'll take it home," I mutter to myself and then return to cleansing the area. I sprinkle fresh salt in all four corners and recharge my wards.

Xander's right. We need to reset all the protection tools we have. And I admit, I've not been as vigilant about it here in the shop as I should have been.

That all changes now.

It's later than I want when I finally walk through the back door of my house, but it took me a long time to make sure the shop was safe.

I muscle the large piece of labradorite onto a table in the living room and then set off in search of my girl.

I find her in her spinning space, hunched over the wheel, threading wool to make yarn.

She's surrounded by the stuff, bags and bags of it, all separated by color and scattered across the floor. Merlin's lying atop one of the bags, napping away.

Breena's blonde hair is disheveled, coming out of the ponytail she secured early this morning. She has shadows under her eyes and little cuts on her fingers. She looks fucking exhausted.

"Hey."

Her head comes up, and then she winces and rolls her shoulder.

"Honey, you've been sitting there all day."

"I know," she says and then clears her throat. "I have the cankles to prove it. I never thought I'd have to deal with swollen ankles before I even turn thirty, but I guess that's what sitting at this thing all day gets me."

"You need a break."

"But I'm almost done with this part. I want to start weaving tomorrow, and—"

"Break," I repeat and move toward her. Taking her hand in mine, I pull her up to her feet. Once she's untangled herself from the spinner, I cup her face in my hands and kiss the hell out of her.

She still smells like sunshine and feels like heaven, and when I pull back, I can't help but rest my forehead against hers and just be still with her.

"Needed that all day," I whisper.

"I guess I did, too." Her hands are on my sides, loosely hanging on. It's taken every fiber of willpower over the past couple of weeks to keep the physical affection to just this. To not take it much, *much* further with her because we have so much hanging over our heads.

There's a lot at stake.

I'm not a young man. I don't have to let my dick lead the way every minute of every day.

But damn, I want her every minute of every day. I want to make her mine in every sense of the word.

I've always been a patient man, but even I have limits.

"What are you thinking about so hard?" she finally asks.

"Nothing." I kiss her forehead and then back away.

"Did you have a bad day?"

"No, it was actually a good business day."

"And the rest?"

I shrug a shoulder. I don't want to scare her, but I don't want to keep her in the dark either.

"I had some poltergeist activity in the shop today."

"What?" She turns from gathering up the yarn she just spun, her eyes wide with concern. "Is that normal?"

"No, definitely not normal."

She frowns and looks worried, and I shake my head.

"Don't worry. I cleansed everything really well. That's why I'm later than usual tonight."

"I didn't even notice the time," she admits and takes a deep breath, pressing her hands into the small of her back and stretching. "The only break I took today was to make some bread."

"You baked fresh bread?" I sniff the air and smile. "You *did*."

"Do you know how many preservatives are in the bread you buy at the store? I'm not eating that. But a girl needs carbs."

"A guy does, too."

She grins. "Exactly."

"You know what else you need?"

She bites her lip the way she does when she's nervous, and my stomach clenches. "What?"

"A massage. Come on, that back of yours is in knots. I can see it from here. I have some arnica salve I got from Lucy's shop—"

"Oh, I forgot to get some of that."

"—and you're going to lie down and let me rub it into those overworked muscles."

"Does that mean I have to get naked?"

I stop and watch her, trying to gauge the correct answer.

"The arnica works better directly *on* the skin."

"Right." She worries that lip again and then nods

before walking out of the room ahead of me. "Where are we doing this?"

"My bedroom is fine. The arnica is in there."

"Right."

She stands at the end of the bed like a woman going to the guillotine.

"Sweetheart, if you don't want me to touch you like that, we can skip it. Instead, take a nice, hot bath to loosen up. That'll work."

"No." She swallows hard and looks at the bed. "No, a massage sounds really nice. Arnica is just what I need."

Rather than reach for the salve, I sit on the edge of the bed and wait for her to look me in the eye. When she does, I offer her a smile.

"Hi."

"Hello," she replies and licks her lips.

"Why are you so nervous about a back rub?"

She shrugs sharply. "I'm not."

"Lie."

Her eyes find mine again, and then she blows out a gusty sigh. "I don't know why I'm nervous. Maybe because I haven't taken my shirt off in front of a man in a really, *really*—" She scrunches up her nose, and I want to kiss it. "Wait. I've never done that."

"I'm sorry, what?"

"I've never taken my shirt off in front of a man."

Everything in me stills. She can't be serious. She can't be almost thirty and still a virgin.

"I'm not a virgin," she hurries on as if she can read my mind. "But it wasn't...you know. *Fun.*"

"That's almost worse." I drag my hand down my face in agitation. Not at *her*. No, she's done nothing wrong. But the asshole—or assholes—who got to have sex with this woman and didn't make it fun for her? They need a hexing spell, STAT. "Okay, so here's what we're going to do. I'm going to leave the room so you can remove as much clothing as you feel comfortable taking off. I mean that. Then, you're going to get under the covers of that bed, on your belly."

She nods, glancing at the bed again.

"When I come back in, I'll peel the covers down only as far as your lower back. I'll rub your shoulders, neck, and back. Probably your arms. I won't be able to see anything you don't want me to."

"I think that sounds like a good idea."

I nod but reach for her and gently kiss her sweet lips when I stand. "You're safe here, Breena."

She offers me a small smile, then I leave the room and close the door behind me. While she undresses, I walk to the kitchen, warm up a rice bag in the microwave, wash my hands, and set a pot of water on to boil.

Finally, armed with a tray, I make my way back to the bedroom. I set the hot teapot and cups on the table by the bed and rest the rice bag over the covers, down Breena's spine.

She lets out a long, happy sigh.

In the bathroom, I find the salve. When I return to

the bedroom, I turn the lights low and move the rice bag to Breena's low back so I can move the covers.

"This is nice," she murmurs softly. "Don't let me fall asleep. I don't want to miss anything."

"Okay." I pull back the blankets and find that she has stripped down to her skin. She didn't even leave her bra on.

My dick decides to sit up and take notice.

She has a lean back with two dimples down low, tempting me to find out what's hiding farther down.

But a promise is a promise, so I rub some salve between my hands and get to work, starting with her shoulders and then moving my way down and across her shoulder blades, her rib cage, and to her low back before gliding my hands up either side of her spine back to her neck.

She moans softly, sending another zing of electricity through me.

Maybe this was a bad idea. I don't plan to make any sexy moves on her until after we've solved the mysteries we're working on. I don't want to put any more pressure on her than what she already has.

But damn, it's hard.

Pun intended.

Finally, I make my way down her arms to her fingertips and then cover her again and move away from her.

"Wait," she says, surprising me. "You forgot a spot."

I raise an eyebrow. "I did?"

"Uh-huh." She turns over onto her back and smiles at

me, but then uncertainty makes its way into those stunning eyes.

"What is it?"

"Giles, I'm confused."

I sit next to her. "Why?"

"Are you *ever* going to make love to me? Or is that not what we have going on here?"

CHAPTER TEN
BREENA

He licks his lips, and I think maybe I said the wrong thing. My stomach sinks, and I move to leave the bed, but he stops me, his hand on mine. "I've been trying to wait."

"For what?" I frown, not understanding. "An invitation? Well, you have one. An open one."

I don't know that I've ever seen Giles so nervous before. Shocked, yes, but never nervous. He licks his lips and pushes his glasses up his nose, and I suddenly feel bad.

"I'm not trying to rush you," I say softly. "If you're not ready, it's okay. You're just always so affectionate, and I see how you look at me sometimes. I just thought maybe..."

My voice tapers off, and I feel stupid.

"Not ready?" He clears his throat and then laughs,

making me feel even *more* stupid, if that's even possible. "Honey, I've been ready for a long time. I just didn't want to add any more pressure on you."

"By all means. Add some pressure. But I have to warn you; I'm not very good at this stuff."

"I'm going to show you just how wrong that statement is." It's a promise. One I can't wait to see how he goes about following through on.

"I think you should take off some of your clothes."

For the love of all the gods and goddesses, I *so* want to see him naked. I've wanted it since I was fourteen and realized Giles was the one for me. I didn't know how I knew; I just *did*.

He's so tall and broad and has muscles that seem to go on for days. Is that from all the rocks he hauls around? Maybe. Whatever it is, thank the gods for it.

"Your eyes look...greedy," he decides, and I immediately nod.

"I don't know how to play coy or hard to get," I confess, feeling totally lame. "I never did master that feminine skill."

"Good." He stands and unbuttons his blue shirt, uncovering smooth skin and abs that should be on the cover of a men's health magazine. "I don't want you to play games with me, Breena. If you want me, I want to know about it."

"Same goes," I mutter before he drops the shirt to the floor and then crawls onto the bed. "Pants?"

"If I strip down to the skin right now, I'll be inside you in about ten seconds flat, and I want to take my time exploring you."

I pause. Is that even a thing? Don't guys just climb on top, stick it in, and the next thing you know, they're snoring, and you're questioning your life choices?

Giles narrows his eyes. "I see we have some fun work ahead of us."

"Okay."

He chuckles once more, but I don't feel stupid this time. No, I'm just excited to see what comes next.

With the flick of his finger, the candle beside the bed comes to life, and I feel my eyes widen in surprise.

"I didn't know you could do that one."

"I can do a lot," he confesses as he lowers his head to brush his nose across mine. "I just don't show it off much."

"I want to know what else you can do."

"Oh, I think I'm about to show you."

That makes me laugh, but it turns to a sigh when he drifts down to nibble just below my ear. It feels magical.

Giles peels back the covers and joins me under them as he continues to kiss my neck, moving down to my collarbone. He doesn't nibble lower to my breasts, though.

Instead, he kisses his way up to my lips and sinks in as if he needs to feast on me. My hands find their way up his naked back, and I simply let myself *enjoy* him in a way I've never been able to enjoy a man before.

There's no rush here. No need to hurry. Instead, it feels like time has stopped altogether, and we can just lazily soak each other in.

His hand finally grazes up my side to my breast, where he gently worries the nipple between his fingers. I arch my back, inviting him to do more.

"Goddess above, you're so fucking sweet," he murmurs against my lips. "So damn soft and sweet. I'm telling you right now, if you don't want or like anything I do, all you have to do is tell me, and I'll stop."

"Don't want you to stop."

"Look at me."

I open my eyes, and there he is, those intense eyes gazing down at me fiercely.

"Just tell me to stop, okay?"

"I will." But I know deep in the marrow of my bones that I won't want him to stop. No way.

But with that promise, Giles kisses his way down my body and then freezes.

"You got *naked*." His eyes find mine again, his expression full of surprise now.

"You told me to undress as far as I felt comfortable."

"Well, yeah. But I thought...never mind. It doesn't matter. It was just a pleasant surprise, that's all." His hand glides over the outside of my hip and down to my thigh. I sigh in pleasure. "Your body is amazing, Breen."

"I'm already naked, Giles. You don't have to—"

I break off when he bites my inner thigh.

"I'm not placating you to get inside you. No games

here, remember?" He licks over the tender flesh where his teeth were, and I sigh. "You cover all these spectacular curves with dresses and cloaks."

"I'm a witch," I remind him.

"Not all witches wear all those clothes."

"This one does." I gasp when his lips skim across that tenderest spots where my leg meets my most private place. "Oh, my gods."

My fingers dive into his thick, dark hair, and when his tongue begins to work a kind of magic I never even knew existed, I can't help but cry out.

My body is no longer mine as it bows and tightens, my breath coming fast and my spine starting to tingle.

"This is insane."

But he doesn't stop. Before long, I feel myself come apart, just freaking *come apart* in a way I didn't know existed.

"Wow."

I can't breathe quite yet, so that's all I can say.

But I feel Giles kissing his way up my body, and if I'm not mistaken, I feel *wind*.

"Is the window open?" I ask him.

"No, baby, that's *you*. You conjured up one hell of a windstorm in here."

My eyes fly open, and I gaze around. The lampshade is tilted, and papers are scattered. It *does* look like a storm blew through.

"Oh, I'm so sorry."

"Never be sorry for that." He covers my mouth with his once more, and I can taste myself on him. At first, it feels scandalous, but it makes me feel so sexy and *desired* I fear I'll crave it all the time now.

He pins one of my hands with his over my head and nudges my legs apart so he can rest between them.

"When did you take your pants off?" I hear myself say.

"I worked them down while you were losing yourself in the most spectacular of ways." He smiles down at me, brushes a piece of my hair off my cheek, and kisses me lightly. "How are you, beautiful?"

"I'm not sure if I've ever been better, actually."

That smile grows, and he tips his forehead against mine. "That's good to hear. You know, once we do this next part, there's no going back, so I want to make sure you're sure."

"So sure. Never been more sure about anything in my life."

"Thank the goddess." He slips inside me, slowly. So painfully slow that I think I might die from it. "Holy shit, you're tight."

"I think you're just well-endowed, Giles."

He doesn't laugh as I intended. Instead, he squeezes his eyes shut and mutters, "Spaghetti."

"I beg your pardon?"

"Baseball. Snow drifts."

"What are you doing?"

"Trying to think of things that will help me not come as fast as my dick wants to."

I laugh, and he groans.

"Laughing only makes it worse because you tighten around me when you do that."

"Really?" I try it again and feel my muscles squeeze around him. Then I do it without the laughter, and Giles hisses out a breath. "Oh, this is fun."

I shift my hips, tightening as the movement makes him slide out of me just a bit. He slides back in when I move the other way, and the sensation is simply delicious.

"This is really nice," I inform him.

"Killing me," he mutters, but then he starts moving with me, and I feel the wind kicking up around us again as the tension builds between us.

I can't get enough. He moves faster, pumps harder, and I meet him with every thrust until we both reach the peak together, clinging to each other and riding out the ecstasy of it all.

Breathing hard, Giles collapses on top of me, buries his face in my neck, and says, "Whoa."

A door slams down the hall, but neither of us moves.

"My house, Molly," Giles calls out. "You don't like it? You can move out."

The door slams once more, and we laugh together as we disentangle ourselves from each other. Giles leans on his elbow and looks down at me.

"You okay?"

"I'm great. Who knew it was that fun?"

He smiles softly and leans down to kiss me gently. "We're going to find lots of fun things to do together."

"I'll hold you to that." I drag my fingers down his face and see *more* in his eyes. More than affection. More than friendship.

It returns the hope I made myself let go of months ago.

"What is it?" He whispers the question.

"It's really nice to have something good to hold on to in the middle of the madness we're living right now."

"Yeah." He sighs and looks grim for a moment. "I'm sorry it's happening this way."

"I'm not."

He raises an eyebrow.

"I'm not sorry, Giles. If it weren't happening, just like this, we might not have found each other. I'd have my little crush, and you'd be doing your thing, and it might never have become anything at all."

"I don't believe that." He shakes his head and moves to sit, bracing his elbows on his knees. I sit next to him, tucking the sheet under my arms. "We would have ended up here sooner or later. When it's meant to be, it finds a way, Breena."

"And do you believe that? That we're meant to be?"

His eyes narrow on my face as he reaches out to frame it with his hands.

"I know, without a doubt, that you were made to be

mine. That we were meant to live this life together. And that's what I intend to do."

He's so *sure* that I can't help but grin at him.

"Maybe I shouldn't have been so embarrassed when Lorelei told you I've been in love with you all my life."

"I hate that you were," he says. "Embarrassed, that is. How do you feel now?"

I remember what we said about no games, so I square my shoulders and lift my chin. "I realize that what I felt for you before was absolutely a crush. I was enamored with and attracted to you. But now? Now that I've spent so much time with you and worked alongside you, I can say without a shadow of a doubt that I'm completely in love with you, Giles Corey."

There's no great leap of joy with my confession. No passionate embrace or scream of excitement.

He simply takes my hand, kisses my knuckles, and then finds my gaze with his.

"I love you, too. And I will love you for as long as there's life in me, Breena."

"**K**eep that hood on."

Jonas circles me, taking in the outfit Lucy helped me put together for my journey over the bridge that separates Salem from Hallows End.

"I might not need this," I remind everyone. "Jonas's

clothes change with the times when he comes and goes out of the village."

"Mine did, too," Lucy says with a nod. "But we don't want to chance it. If for some reason your clothes don't change and someone sees you, we don't want you freaking them out with your modern clothing."

"I wish the invisibility spell was a real thing," I mutter. "Or that I could shift like Xander and just fly through as a bird."

"We have to go if you want to see the village before nightfall," Jonas says.

"Be careful," Giles tells me before I can walk away. He frames my face and kisses me hard. "Be *very* careful."

"We will." I smile reassuringly, not sure who I'm trying to convince, him or me.

"Come." Jonas holds out his hand for mine, and I take it. I feel the energy shift as soon as we reach the bridge.

"Wow, Jonas."

"I know."

We walk over, and halfway there, it's like moving through a force field. A bright light. Suddenly, we're over the bridge, and I'm staring at a little town I've never seen before.

"Come. Over to the tree line." Jonas leads me into a little copse. "Hide here for a moment while I do a quick walk-through to ensure it's safe."

I nod and do as I'm told, clinging to a trunk.

I know what houses from the sixteen hundreds

looked like from history lessons, but seeing them in real life is amazing.

They're one-room, dark gray buildings. Very small, with chimneys that climb one wall. They even have thatched roofs.

I see livestock in fenced yards. Wagons and horses.

But I don't see any people. They must all be inside for dinner, which makes sense since it's late in the day.

Finally, Jonas comes hurrying back and gestures for me to follow him.

"I don't have to go far," I tell him. "I already have some great ideas just from this."

"Good." He swallows hard, and I can tell this is incredibly stressful for him. "Let's hurry. My house is at the edge of town. We can stop by there quickly."

"Oh, I'd love to see your home."

Jonas is a tall man, so I have to hurry to keep up with his long strides. I'm taking it all in, down to the color of the trees, grass, and dirt roads. When he pulls me into his house, I let out a long breath.

"This is incredible." I wander to his fireplace and am not surprised at all when it comes to life without the help of matches. Jonas is gifted with fire. "This cauldron is beautiful." I run a finger over the pot hanging above the flames.

"It's six hundred years old," he informs me.

"Wow."

"It's a modest home. They all are. Some have more

rooms for privacy if the family is larger, but they're all very simple."

"Where do you go to the bathroom?"

Jonas laughs. "There's an outhouse."

"Yikes. I mean, I *know* there was no plumbing then. But, man. Not fun."

"If you've never had it, you don't miss it."

I turn and look at him. "You're right. Jonas, I'm so happy we have you. That you found your way to us. I know you and Lucy are meant to be, but you mean a lot to all of us. Including me."

"You are the sweetest woman I've ever met, Breena. I love you, too. And I'm blessed to be welcomed into your family. No matter what happens, I want you to remember that."

"We're going to solve this. We *are.*"

He smiles, but it doesn't reach his eyes, and we both know it's impossible for me to make that promise. We'll do our best, but I can't know for certain that it will be good enough.

"Come, we're losing light."

I nod and wait for Jonas to make sure the coast is still clear before hurrying out with him and returning to the bridge.

When we're back in modern times, Jonas and I both take long, relieved breaths.

"You did it!" Lucy says, clapping her hands. "Are you both okay?"

"I'm great," I reply. "And I don't think anyone saw us. Wow, it's such a beautiful little village. I can't believe it's only twenty yards away, right over there, and we can't see it."

"I know," Lucy agrees. "I've lived here forever and never knew it was there."

"Do you have what you need?" Xander asks me.

"I do." I nod and look over at Jonas, then move to give him a hug. "Thank you. It was exactly what I needed. And now I feel confident in designing the tapestry and getting started with the weaving."

"I'm glad," Jonas says. "I know you'll do a wonderful job."

"You're sure you're okay?" Giles asks, taking my shoulders in his hands.

"Yes, I'm sure. It was completely amazing. A little disconcerting going through that bright light and feeling the energy shift, but really cool."

I glance over and see Lorelei and Lucy sharing a look.

"What?" I demand.

"Nothing," Lucy says immediately, but Lorelei doesn't respond.

"What is it?" I ask her.

"You two seem different," Lorelei says, and Lucy rolls her eyes.

"Different how?" I ask, but I know.

"Like you've had sex and are gonna get married and grow old together."

"*Lorelei*," Lucy hisses.

"Oh, I'm totally banging him," I reply and watch

everyone's eyes widen in surprise. "Not that it's anyone's business, of course. But, yeah. Totally banging him."

"Well, then." Lucy tries unsuccessfully to hide a laugh behind her hand. "Good for you."

"You have no idea."

CHAPTER ELEVEN
GILES

"Oh, my. Mrs. Boksich is going to love that." Mom leans over and watches as I set a three-karat ruby into a fourteen-karat-gold setting. "What a gorgeous fiftieth-anniversary gift."

"Mr. Boksich said the ruby belonged to his grandmother," I tell her as I sit back and roll my shoulders, trying to loosen the tension there. "It was in a broken brooch, so we decided to reset it and shine it up for her. The anniversary party is tomorrow night, and I'm trying to get it finished for him."

"So that's why you're working on the one day a week you usually close the shop," Mom says with a nod. "Well, that's very sweet of you, and I know they'll appreciate it. I've always liked that family. Not a witchy bone in any of their bodies, but they're as sweet as can be."

"I like them, too." I sip my long-cold coffee and smile

at my mom. "Not that I'm complaining, but did you just swing by to say hello?"

"Yes, and to bring you this." She opens her bag, which is big enough to carry a few Saint Bernard puppies and pulls out a brown paper sack with my name written on the side like she used to do when I was a kid. She sets it on the counter. "I made some donuts this morning."

"Really?" I open the bag and take a long, deep breath full of sugar and yeast. "Score. Thanks. I forgot to eat breakfast. Breena was already at work at the loom this morning, so I snuck out. I didn't want to disturb her. She gets really intense when she's working."

"She knows how important this task is," Mom says. "How is she?"

"Scared." I take a bite of a donut. "I hate seeing her afraid, but she is. Mostly of the thought that she might fail and we'll lose because of her. That scares her the most."

"Breena is a pleaser," Mom reminds me. "It's always been in her nature to want to help and nurture others. I know she's excited that she has a skill that can aid in lifting the curse, but it makes sense she'd be afraid of failing. That must be stressful for her."

"It is. And all I can do is try to reassure her that nothing is her fault."

"And love her."

Mom smiles when my gaze whips up to hers.

"You're my only child, Giles. Do you honestly think I don't see what's happening between the two of you? And for the record, I'm a fan. I love Breena to the moon and back. She's perfect for you. You're excellently balanced, and I can't wait to hold my grandchildren."

"Whoa." I laugh and hold up my hands in surrender. "You're skipping a few steps there, Mom."

"The sentiment is the same." She shrugs a shoulder. "How is the tapestry coming along?"

"Well, since Breena went with Jonas into Hallows End last week, she's been working quickly. It took her a few days to sketch out what she wants the scene to look like, but now that she has figured that out and Jonas approved it, she's getting started with the actual weaving and stitching. I think it's harder than any of us realizes."

"I think you're right," Mom says, tapping her finger against her lips. "I'll swing by the house on my way home to see if she needs any help. Even if that just means making her a pot of tea and something to snack on."

"Get her to walk around a bit," I suggest. "She's been sitting so much her ankles have started to swell."

Mom frowns. "That's not healthy. I'll see what I can do for her. I have some alfalfa caplets with me."

"Of course, you do."

"What does that mean?"

"Nothing." I laugh and kiss my mother on the cheek. "Just that you're such a kitchen witch. You carry medicinal herbs around with you everywhere you go."

"Do you need some elderberry tincture? I have some of that with me, too."

"No thanks." I walk her to the door so I can lock it behind her. "Have a good day. Thanks for the donuts."

"You're welcome. Don't work too hard on your day off."

She kisses my cheek and then sets off. I close and lock the door and then return to my work in progress. Before sitting, I turn on some music so it isn't quite so quiet. As classic Def Leppard fills the air, I get back to it.

Two hours later, with the ring finished, boxed, and ready for Mr. Boksich to pick up first thing in the morning, I turn off the music and start cleaning up my space. I'm ready to get home to Breena and see how she's doing and also find out what I can do to help.

But after I get the ring in the safe and turn to reach for my keys, I hear footsteps above me. Goose bumps spring up all over my body.

I haven't rented out the apartment upstairs. I don't think I'm going to. I figured I'd use it for storage and maybe a space to fill online orders once I get that new part of my business up and running.

No one should be up there.

Blowing out a breath, I tuck my keys into my pocket, lock the shop door, set the alarm, and then climb the stairs to the apartment above.

"Hello?" I call out as I unlock the door, using the keypad. "Is someone squatting up here? That's not cool."

But when I walk inside the empty space, no one is there. There are no signs that anyone has been in the apartment since we moved Breena out weeks ago. It's dusty, and I'm reminded that I should really come up and open a window now and again to air out the place.

I move to walk into the kitchen when I see a shadow figure out of the corner of my eye. When I turn toward it, it's gone.

Well, damn.

I'm not a seer. It wasn't until very recently that I'd ever seen a spirit for myself. Sometimes, I can hear things. And other times, I just *know* when something's there, but I don't see them.

Until all of this started with the curse and the killer.

I saw what was happening at Breena's house.

And now, this.

I backtrack down the stairs to the shop and find a bundle of herbs, light it, and return upstairs to cleanse the space.

But when I walk inside, I see it's fully furnished, but not with modern furniture. All the kitchen appliances are *old*. Something simmers on the stove, and music comes from the bedroom. I can hear the static of a record player.

"Hello?"

My stomach clenches when a little boy walks out of the bedroom holding a knife dripping with thick, red blood.

"She was bad," he says. His eyes are black, and his voice sounds like an echo from far away. "Really bad."

"Who was?" I ask, then watch as his face changes. Remembering the burning herbs in my hand, I begin the chant I always use when I'm cleansing a space. This isn't real. *He* isn't real. "Only love and light are welcome here."

The little face crumples into an expression of rage, and the boy shifts into a man—a tall one who moves to advance on me. I stand my ground and continue talking.

"Anything that is not for my highest good must leave." It's growling now, avoiding the smoke from the bundle. "Did you hear me, asshole? Get the fuck out of here."

It roars in anger, but when I advance with the smoke and clear intentions, it rushes to the window and leaves.

The room changes back to the empty apartment that was here earlier.

And yet, I feel a tingling in my shoulders that tells me I'm not alone.

The growling begins behind me. When I turn, I see a dog. A red one with human eyes, its teeth bared.

"Fuck this." I raise my hands, trace a sigil in the air, and begin a banishing and warding spell. "Evil hiding in plain sight, I use this spell with all my might. To banish your form and vanquish your hate, this chant today will seal your fate."

It snarls and then runs out the door. I move to follow, but something shoves me from behind, and then everything goes dark.

"I think he's waking up."

I hear Breena's whisper. She's here? She must have come to the shop to see me.

My eyes blink open, and I see she's not alone. Jonas frowns at me, holding a stethoscope to my chest. Breena peers down at me over his shoulder.

"Hi," she says with a forced smile. "Welcome back."

I move to sit up, but Jonas pushes me back down. "Stay still. You have a concussion."

"No, I just tripped over something. I need to get home."

They exchange a worried glance.

"You *are* home, Giles." Breena moves away, and I hear her pouring something into a glass. "Here, you need some water."

"Just a minute," Jonas says once more as he shines a light in my eyes. "Better than yesterday."

"*Yesterday?*" I stare at him as if he's gone mad. "What are you talking about? I just fell down a few minutes ago."

"Two days," Breena says and bites her lower lip. "We found you above the shop two days ago. There was a fire."

"What?" I sit up, ignoring Jonas. "Is my shop gone? Just tell me."

"No. It was only a small fire from the cleansing bundle you had with you upstairs. It set off the smoke alarm, and someone got there before it caused any real damage."

"Thank the gods." I lay down again and will my heart rate to slow. "Oh, shit! Mr. Boksich needs his ring."

"I spoke with him," Breena assures me. "It's fine. Everything is okay."

But it doesn't feel okay.

It feels *off*.

"Who are you, really?"

Breena and Jonas share a look, and then Breena's gone, and it's just Jonas looking down at me. His lips pull into a sinister smile.

"You're going to die," he says.

"Giles!"

I open my eyes and stare up into Xander's face.

"If you're not *really* Xander, I'm going to lose my shit."

"It's me," he says, kneeling next to me. "What happened?"

"Fell." I sit up, and the room spins. "I think I need to get out of here."

"Let's go."

"I had a lit herb bundle." I look around and find that it burned itself out. I grab it, and Xander helps me to my feet and down the stairs. "I don't like that it's trying to fuck with me in my shop."

"I don't either," he says grimly. "Let's get you home."

"No." I stop. Now that I'm outside and in the fresh air, I feel much more *with it*. Not dizzy. Not disoriented.

"It keeps trying to disorient me. Like it wants to confuse me."

"That's pretty much on par for this thing."

"Yeah. But I'm not about to be scared out of my own business, Xander. This is *mine*. I'm not going anywhere."

"What do you want to do?"

"I want to make it clear, plain as day, that it has no power here."

Xander nods and looks up at the building, then back at me. "Did it touch you?"

I start to say no but then remember that it felt as if something pushed me down. "Maybe. I don't think I fell. I think I was pushed."

"Ballsy little fucker," he mutters. "Okay, we need some supplies and some witches."

"I don't want to call in the coven." I shake my head. "They're already doing a lot."

"There's power in numbers, but I don't think it's necessary to call in the whole coven. We'll just have the other four join us."

"Right now?"

"Right fucking now."

Xander and I reach for our phones and start making calls. I can tell I've pulled Breena out of a working haze, but when I explain what just happened, her eyes clear and narrow on the FaceTime call.

"What do I need to bring?"

"Your besom," Xander says over my shoulder. "We're going to clean house."

"I just made a new one. I'll also bring some floor wash powder and some salt. Oh! And—"

"Breena," Xander says with a smile. "Just bring whatever feels right."

"Okay. Got it. I'll be there in about twenty minutes."

"Lucy and Jonas are on their way," Xander says after Breena hangs up.

"And Lorelei?"

His jaw tightens. "She won't pick up for me."

"Oh, for fuck's sake." I FaceTime Lorelei's number, and she picks up on the second ring, her face comes onto the screen. "You have *got* to stop being so damn stubborn and answer the phone when Xander calls."

"The last time I checked, I was a grown-ass woman who doesn't have to do *anything*."

"I'm going to spank her," I hear Xander whisper and choose not to share that with Lorelei.

"We need your help." I give her all the information and watch as her eyes transform from annoyance to concern.

"On my way. Be there in twenty."

She cuts off, and I tuck my phone into my pocket.

"We can get any crystals we need out of the shop. I don't have a broom here, though. Not a magic one, anyway."

"Any broom will do," he says with a smile, but the grin drops when we hear growling behind us.

"Here we go again."

We turn and find the red dog with its human eyes.

"Your bravery doesn't scare us," Xander says, making it growl louder. It crouches like it's about to strike, but then it stops, whimpers, and walks away.

"Good boy," Lucy says, petting Nera on the back. "He scared that thing off. The first time we saw it, it spooked my boy, but now it just pisses him off."

"Good boy," I croon and scratch the big dog behind his ears. "You're a *very* good boy."

He leans into me as Breena and Lorelei arrive, and I lead everyone upstairs to the apartment.

"I'll be right there," Xander says, turning to the shop. "I'm going to grab some crystals."

"Whatever you need," I assure him with a nod before climbing the steps with the others.

"Someone's here," Lorelei says immediately, narrowing her eyes and walking in a circle around the empty space of the living room. Suddenly, she turns to me. "And you fell. Right here."

"Yeah, I did. Something pushed me and knocked me out."

"I never had any encounters when I lived here," Breena adds as Xander joins us, carrying crystals in both of his huge hands. "It was always quiet."

"Yeah, well, something moved in after you moved out," Lucy says and closes her eyes. "It's angry."

"Is it *it*?" I ask. "The killer entity?"

"No," Breena says before anyone else can reply. "No, I'd feel it. I don't know how I know that. I just do."

"I have a question," Lorelei says, turning to Xander.

"How is it that *you're* always the one nearby when something happens to Giles? It happened the other day, too, when he had the vision of being in 1692. And now this. How?"

"I'm psychic," Xander reminds her. "And I happened to be nearby. The first time, I was walking by and saw him completely by happenstance."

"And this time?" Lorelei demands.

"I was flying by," Xander responds, "and saw in the window."

"Do you often peek in people's windows? Because that's just wrong. I never took you for a peeping Tom, but I guess after all the shit you've pulled, it wouldn't surprise me."

"So, are we just going to be mean to each other, or are we going to do something about whatever is tormenting Giles?" Breena asks, cutting into the argument. "Because I have stuff I could be doing at home."

"Wow." Lorelei smiles over at her cousin. "I like that you're becoming more outspoken lately."

"I don't have time to be anything else," Breena reminds her and then turns to me. "You and I aren't mediums, but even I can feel that something's wrong here."

"Yeah, that's why I came up to investigate earlier. I heard footsteps while I was working downstairs. Part of me hoped it was a squatter."

"What is a squatter?" Jonas asks, frowning at his wife. "That's a term I have not heard before."

"You know, a homeless person who breaks into a place and lives there uninvited, rent free," Xander says. "A squatter."

"Ah. Yes, that makes sense. And would be more convenient in this case."

"But, no." I sigh and prop my hands on my hips. "It's some weird shit."

"We live in Salem," Breena reminds me and pats my shoulder. "We're used to weird sh—stuff."

I smile down at her. It's adorable how she doesn't like to swear. "You have a point."

"So, what's the plan? Why did I bring my besom? I just made it, so please tell me I don't have to ruin it," Lorelei says, holding her tall broom by the handle.

"I just made mine, too," Breena says with a grin. "I love the flowers you used. And the shells. Did you find those on your shoreline?"

"Can we discuss besom embellishments another time?" Lucy asks her cousins. "We have some spirits to scare off here."

"Oh, right," Breena says, returning her attention to Xander. "Sorry. What do we do?"

"Sweep," Xander replies.

"That's it?" I ask him.

"It's a start."

CHAPTER TWELVE
BREENA

"This place shines," Lorelei says. We just spent the past hour sweeping, cleaning, and speaking spells aloud to keep the negative energy away.

"I felt it," I say and look toward the open window. "I felt it leave. Was I imagining things?"

"No," Lucy says. "I felt it, too. When Giles placed that last crystal in the corner."

Xander closes the window, and we all stare at the pile of dust in the center of the room.

"We have to bury that," Jonas says, and Xander nods in agreement.

"But where?" I ask. "It shouldn't be where any of us lives."

"What if we bury it at your old place?" Lorelei suggests, looking at me. "You certainly don't live there anymore—and don't plan to."

"But there's already so much activity there," I reply with a frown. "Wouldn't this fuel that?"

"I don't think so," Jonas puts in. "This is charged with *our* magic, not that of whatever we just got rid of. At the very least, I think it's neutral. Best case, it has a positive effect on what's happening at the house."

"Agreed," Xander puts in. "But it's your property, Breena. You have the final say in that, and there's no pressure."

"As long as we don't think it'll make things worse, I'm fine with it. Let's do it."

Giles secures the apartment, double-checks the locks on Gems' doors, and then we're off to my property.

"I'm riding with you," Giles says. "You're not going there alone, even if it is just for a few moments. I can pick up my car later."

"Thank you." I don't even bother putting up any kind of argument. I *want* him with me.

We're the first to arrive, and I park farther back from the house than I normally would. The others follow suit, pulling up behind and beside me. When we get out of the vehicles, we form a half-circle, facing the house.

Xander's holding the bag of dirt from the apartment.

"Where should we bury it?" I ask and swallow hard.

"Anywhere," Lorelei says. "There is some crazy shit happening in that house."

Her eyes track something moving about, making all the hair on my body stand on end.

"I've never seen anything like it," Jonas adds and instinctively wraps his arm around Lucy.

"What happened here opened a portal," Xander says at last, and I'm shocked to hear apprehension in his voice, even for a second. Xander is the strongest, most self-assured witch I know. To know that this has him unnerved is startling.

"I can't see it," I reply. "But when Giles and I came here a few weeks ago to get my loom, I saw shadows."

"We need to do this and get out of here," Lucy says. "Where do you want to put it?"

"We're on the property now," I tell them. "We can simply put it right here."

"Great. Where's the shovel?" Giles asks.

"I have one in that shed." I point to the side of the house. Before anyone can respond, Xander shifts into his crow form and flies to the shed, then shifts back and walks inside. Seconds later, he returns, carrying the shovel and walking briskly.

"The shed seems to be quiet," he informs us and immediately begins digging a hole in the grass. It doesn't have to be big, so it doesn't take long. We empty the dirt into the hole, and then Xander covers the debris and fills it in again.

"Are you okay?" Lorelei asks Xander, her voice the softest I've heard it where he's concerned in a very long time.

"We need to get out of here," he replies. "It's not safe for any of us."

Xander turns to me and grips my shoulders.

"You won't ever come here alone again. And as soon as possible, this place needs to be sold."

"I can't sell it until we cleanse it."

"Part of the problem is that you *own* it," he replies. "Once it's no longer connected to you, to any of us, this will all go away."

I look back at the house and feel sadness and grief fill my chest.

"I loved this little house," I whisper and feel a tear land on my cheek. "It was my dream house. It was everything I ever wanted. Now, it's haunting those I love."

I shake my head and turn my face up to Xander.

"I'll sell it. I'm sorry it hurts you."

He's lost some color and doesn't look well at all.

"Come," Jonas says. "Let's go."

Xander immediately shifts back into his crow and flies off, pointed away from the cottage and toward the sea.

Lorelei looks concerned as she watches him. "He needs the sea air to clear his mind. He'll be okay."

"Let's go," Giles echoes, and the rest of us pile into cars and drive away from the house I once loved.

I needed a little break from the loom today. Now that all the yarn is spun, I'm back at the loom, weaving. I enjoy it, but I needed some time away from it to clear my mind.

So, Merlin and I are working in the craft room, filling some orders and making candles. It's my happy place.

"Hey, you little thief." I laugh and take the wick that Merlin found to play with away from him, returning it to the pile. "You always did like to steal the wicks. Okay, we have close to twenty orders to fill, and I'd like to make forty candles so I have them ready to go for future orders."

I love the feel of the room with all its windows that let in so much light. I feel a little guilty that Giles gave up his sunroom for me, but then again, it was empty when I arrived.

He didn't use it anyway.

To make the space look bigger, Giles brought in a beautiful, antique mirror his mother gave him and placed it in the corner. It has golden, gilded edges and stands on an easel so it's high enough to see yourself in and tips up just ever so slightly. It adds light *and* the illusion of space, and I enjoy it.

As the wax slowly melts for the candles, I print off all the packing slips for the orders and grab the baskets I use to set each order in before packaging and shipping.

It's been the easiest way for me to keep everything straight.

"This person bought quite a lot," I inform Merlin, reading the packing slip. "And she wants me to choose some things for her intuitively, which is always fun. I don't know why, but I think she needs a new tarot deck, so we'll toss one of those in there, as well."

I make my way down the shelves Giles built for my stock and pull the items from the slip, setting them in the basket.

And then I do the same for the rest of the orders. By the time I'm finished with that, the wax is melted and ready to pour.

It's a steady process of placing the wicks, pouring the wax, then letting them set while I return to the orders. Before the candles are completely dry, I add herbs, crystals, and trinkets to the tops.

"This isn't so bad. I'm not even going to let myself feel guilty for not being at the loom." I wink at Merlin, who blinks back at me, making me smile.

Seeing something out of the corner of my eye, I glance up and grin as a blue jay flies by the window.

But then my gaze lands on the mirror.

I blink. Several seconds later, my reflection blinks.

I *watch* myself blink.

"What the—?"

The image doesn't mirror my actions of taking a step back for several seconds but then follows suit. I'm officially freaked out.

My heart pounds as I reach up to brush my hair out of my face. The reflection doesn't move at all.

In fact, she just watches me.

"Well, this is new." Mentally, I lift my protective shields and watch as the reflection in the mirror smiles at me.

She freaking *smiles*.

I don't run away. Everything in me is telling me to flee, but I refuse to give whatever this is any power over me.

I've had it up to my eyeballs with being afraid.

So, rather than run, I walk right up to the mirror. I'm fascinated when the edges of the glass start to form ice crystals.

They spread until the entire surface is covered, and I can no longer see the reflection at all.

I pull my sleeve over my hand to clear away the ice and then jump when I see what's staring back at me.

The three of us: Lucy, Lorelei, and me, standing hand-in-hand. The daughters of daughters, looking at me with so much pity and sadness that it almost takes my breath away.

"What's wrong?" I ask aloud. I can see my breath in the now-frigid air of the room. "Tell me what to do."

"You're going to fail," they say in unison, in almost a chant. "You're no good, and you're going to fail."

The mirror ices up once more, and for the second time, I clear it away with my sleeve.

But the three women are gone. The sunroom is no longer in the reflection at all. I feel as though I'm gazing out a window, but I have no idea what I'm looking at outside. It's stormy, with big, angry, black clouds, and lightning flashes in the sky. Trees blow in the wind.

I narrow my eyes and look closer, seeing the sea in the distance.

"Lorelei." I hear myself breathe her name as I watch her walk onto the jagged rocks. Her dark auburn hair swirls around her, and she's in a red dress, also billowing in the wind.

"Lorelei!" I yell out for her, wanting desperately to make her hear me. But I know she can't. This isn't real.

None of this is real.

"This is another trick." My voice is a whip of anger. "I'm so sick of what you're doing to confuse me. You don't hold any power here, and that just pisses you right off, doesn't it? Get out. Get out *now*."

I raise my hands and begin a banishing spell. The wind swirls around me as I chant and push all my intention and energy into the spell, driving anything that isn't for my highest good away.

When I've finished, I look back at the mirror and see myself staring back at me.

I raise my arm, and the reflection follows, just as it should.

"What are you doing?"

I whirl, my hand pressed to my chest, and see Giles standing in the doorway, watching me with a frown on his gorgeous face.

"The mirror and I were having some trouble."

He cocks his head to the side. "I'm sorry, what's that?"

"Nothing." I shake my head, but he advances on me and frames my face in his hands.

"What happened, sweets?"

"You use a *lot* of terms of endearment. I think I like that about you."

"You're not going to change the subject that easily. What happened?"

I look back at the mirror and then at Giles. "Well, it felt like something that happens in a bad horror movie. Like, a really, *really* bad one."

"Okay."

I tell him about the reflection, what I saw, and the wind.

But when I look around the room, my papers aren't scattered everywhere. Everything is as it should be, as if nothing at all happened.

"You might not believe me."

"Why wouldn't I believe you?" He leans back against the worktable and braces his hands on either side of his hips. I have to admit, it's a sexy pose.

"Because it sounds ridiculous. And everything here is normal. I probably hallucinated it all. Maybe I'm more exhausted than I thought. Maybe I just need a nap."

"I believe it happened," he replies softly. "I saw Merlin come running out of here. That's why I came looking for you."

"Oh, poor Merlin. I didn't even think about him. Well, crap. Now I'm a bad mom, too."

"Okay, that's enough." Giles reaches for my hand and pulls me to him, wraps his arms around me firmly, and rubs his hands up and down my back. "You're not a bad mom. You just had a weird experience. Merlin can take care of himself. I suspect we'll just have odd things happening for the next little while. Do you feel unsafe in this house?"

"No." I shake my head and tip it back so I can look at him. "I feel perfectly safe here. And while it was happening, I wasn't terrified. I was a little scared at first. Mostly, I was annoyed. Maybe a bit curious. I did a banishing spell, and then it was gone, and everything was back to normal."

"I suspect that it—whatever *it* is—is trying to taunt and scare us, but it has no real power here. We're too strong for it to have any control."

"I agree. I didn't ever feel like I was in real danger."

"That's the most important thing. Because the minute that changes, I'll take you out of here."

"Giles, I suspect that no matter what we do or where we go, it will follow us. This is just what our lives are going to look like for a bit. And I have to finish that tapestry as soon as possible to make it stop."

"Wait." He frowns down at me. "Breena, the tapestry doesn't have anything to do with the killer. The tapestry is for the curse, to lift it and set Hallows End free."

My mouth opens and then closes again. I frown.

"Why do I lump them together so much in my mind? I keep thinking that one is directly related to the other, but you're right. We're dealing with the killer right now. And at the same time, I'm working on the tapestry to hopefully lift the curse on Hallows End. But they're not necessarily the same thing. Does that mean I don't need to have the tapestry finished by Beltane? Because I don't think that's humanly possible. Why am I so confused about this?"

"I don't see why Beltane would be the deadline for that. I would stick to the original Samhain deadline. That seems to be the most important date when it comes to the curse."

"You're right." So much relief fills me that I beam up at Giles. "Oh, thank the goddess. That actually takes a *lot* of pressure off my shoulders."

"I'm glad. I really am. Because you've been working yourself so hard, you're going to get sick. Speaking of that, why are you filling orders? I thought we agreed that I and the others would help with your bills until the tapestry is finished."

"I can't ask you all to do that." He starts to speak, but I cover his lips with my fingers. "I love you all for wanting to do it, but it's too much to ask, Giles. My orders have been cut way back because I stopped running any advertising, so the number of orders coming in is minimal compared to my usual load. They're mostly just regular customers. I can handle this, especially now that I know I have more time. I'll have much more balance in my life."

"If it starts to feel like it's too much, just tell me and back off altogether."

I open my mouth to argue, but he puts his fingers on *my* mouth this time.

"For the next few months, Breena. Not forever."

I simply sigh and nod because I know he's right. If I overdo it, I won't be any help to anyone.

"Did Mr. Boksich pick up his ring this morning?" I ask him.

"Yes, and he was very pleased with it."

"Of course, he was. You're a genius when it comes to jewelry."

"Well, I don't know if I'd call myself a *genius.*"

"I know what I'm talking about." I lift myself onto my toes and gently lay my lips over his. It's a playful kiss, and when I lower back down, he follows me, bending to reach me and take the kiss to the next level of heat that has my bare toes curling on the wool rug under my feet. "You're good at that."

His lips tip up in a satisfied grin. "It takes two to make it work. Are you finished in here for a while?"

I glance at the table. The orders still need to be packed up and labeled, and then I think about the loom upstairs where I should be working. Still, I nod.

"I have a little time. What did you have in mind?"

"Well, it involves far less clothing." To my surprise, he lifts me into his arms and carries me out of the room to the stairs, then begins climbing them with no obvious plan to set me back on my feet. So, I bury my face in his neck and enjoy the ride. "I'd like to get lost in you for a while, Breena. To remember that we're just two human beings who love each other."

"I'm down for that." I lick his neck up to his ear and then tug on the lobe with my teeth. "In fact, I think that sounds like a brilliant idea. See? Genius."

"You're right." He tosses me onto the bed and grins down at me. "I really *am* a genius. Who knew?"

I giggle when he launches himself onto the mattress beside me. "I knew. I knew it this whole time."

CHAPTER THIRTEEN

In all the hundreds of years of his existence, he's never felt freer than he does now. He can feel the power building within him, so much faster than ever before. His strength grows, and he knows he'll be ready to take what he wants by Beltane.

To take what's rightfully *his*.

Hovering in the mirror, he watches her. She thinks she's safe, and for today, that may be true. But she won't be for long.

Soon, she and the others will be his. Their souls will belong to him—as they should be.

As it should have been all along.

They're such fools. He smiles to himself and watches with utter delight as she runs a brush through her hair, humming to herself. She's just so...*comfortable*.

He's going to enjoy making her suffer. Yes, he will take great delight in that.

Very soon.

Chapter Fourteen
Giles

"Are you ready to go?" I poke my head into Breena's bathroom and grin. She's fussing with her hair, and I want to tell her that there's no need for her to do that because I'm just going to mess it up again later, but I restrain myself.

"Yes," she replies as she drops her hands and stares at herself in the mirror. "I hope I'm dressed appropriately because I don't even know where we're going."

"Boston."

She spins and pins me with a surprised stare. "*Boston?* But I'm wearing jeans because you told me to. Shouldn't I be dressed up more if we're going to dinner in the city?"

"No, ma'am." I walk up behind her and smile at her in the mirror as I loop my arms around her waist and rest my chin on her shoulder. "You look perfect. You'll want to be comfortable for what we're doing."

"Just what *are* we doing?"

"I'm not telling." I wink at her in the mirror, then pull away and lead her out of the bathroom. "Are you ever going to move your things into *my* bathroom?"

"No," she says simply. "I like having my own. I can spread out, and I don't have to share any of the space."

"So, even if I eventually talk you into moving in here with me, you'll keep that bathroom? You don't have to do that. I'll switch with you so you have the bigger one."

She stops cold in the hallway, and I bump into her back. I have to grab her shoulders so she doesn't pitch forward and fall.

"Whoa. Warn a guy if you're going to pull the emergency brake, okay?"

She spins and blinks up at me. "You want me to *move in*? Like not just temporarily?"

"Of course." I lean down to nudge her nose with mine. "It would be awkward if my wife lived somewhere else."

"Your-your *wife*." Her face loses all of its color. "Your wife?"

"We're jumping ahead just a little. We'll get to that part later. But, yeah, I want you here with me always. If you hate the house, we can look for something else. I'm pretty easygoing as long as I'm with you."

"I love this house," she whispers, and then my bedroom door slams. "I don't even mind Molly."

"Well, good. I'm glad to hear it."

"I guess I hadn't considered moving in. For good."

"Now you can consider it." I kiss her forehead. "Don't start overthinking it right now. We can discuss it more later. For tonight, we're going to have some fun. Blow off some steam. I think we all need it."

"*All*?" She tips her head to the side. "You're just full of surprises today, aren't you?"

"I try to keep you on your toes. Come on, we'll be late."

Breena makes sure there's plenty of food in Merlin's dish before following me out the back door to my car parked in the driveway.

"We're picking up Lorelei," I inform Breena as I pull onto the street. Lorelei's cottage is on the other side of town, but she's waiting when I pull up. She hurries down to the car and drops into the back seat, plopping her handbag beside her.

"You know, when a man calls me and tells me to get ready to go out but won't tell me where we're going, I usually ignore him."

"Well, I'm so glad you listened this time," I reply with a laugh and get back on the road.

"We're going into Boston, but that's all I know," Breena replies, turning around to look at her cousin. "How are you today?"

"Pretty good, actually. I got two chapters written in my book, which is a lot with all the research I've been doing. And I got a walk-in, too. Then Giles called and told me to get ready to go out, but that was all he said."

"He's in the car with you," I remind her.

"Yeah, I know. So, spill it. Where are we going? Is it just the three of us?"

"No." My lips twitch when I see Lorelei scowling at me in the rearview mirror. "Just trust me. It's *fun*. Something we haven't had much of over the past six months or so."

"Well, that's true enough." Lorelei leans back in the seat and crosses her arms over her chest, looking out the window. "Guys?"

"Yeah?" Breena asks.

I glance in the mirror again, and my skin goes cold.

A man is sitting next to Lorelei. He's old and very clearly dead.

"What? I don't see anything," Breena says as I pull to the side of the road and throw the car into park.

When I turn around, he's gone. But when I look in the mirror, he's there.

"I don't *feel* anyone next to me," Lorelei says carefully. "But I see him in the mirror."

"I do, too," I reply grimly.

"What? What mirror?" Breena leans over to look in the rearview, and her eyes widen. "Oh, for fuck's sake."

"Breena just said fuck," Lorelei whispers. "I'm in an alternate dimension."

Breena starts speaking a banishing spell, getting louder and louder until the man hisses in the mirror and disappears.

"This is getting *so* irritating," Breena mumbles as she settles back into her seat and fastens her seat belt.

"Is this just a normal evening occurrence for you?" Lorelei wants to know as I get back on the road. "Because if so, we need to talk about it. That's just not normal."

"It's been taunting me through mirrors all day," Breena explains. "I'm not scared, but I am pissed off. It's *so* annoying."

"I'm sorry, but are you sure you're my *cousin*, Breena Hazen, the hearth witch who is unnerved by a whole host of things and never, *ever* uses curse words?"

"That's me." Breena turns in her seat to smile sweetly at Lorelei, and I can't help but chuckle. Goddess, she's fucking adorable. "But my patience is wearing thin, and I've learned that you sometimes have to swear. In dire circumstances, of course. I think this qualifies."

"I think you're right." I reach for her hand and bring it to my lips so I can kiss her knuckles. "And, for the rest of the evening, we're not going to think about this asshole who wants to scare us—"

"I think he wants to *kill* us," Lorelei adds, but I keep talking.

"Instead, we're going to have fun and blow off some steam."

Finding the place I'm looking for, I pull into the parking lot next to Lucy's car and cut the engine.

"Lucy and Jonas are here?" Breena asks while clapping her hands in excitement.

"Does that mean Xander is with them?" Lorelei asks.

"Yes. And you're going to be nice because we *all* need this." As we all get out of the car, I pin her with a stern stare. Lorelei sighs with resignation.

"Fine. I'll be...sort of nice."

"That's all we can ask." Breena links her arm through Lorelei's as I lead the ladies into the building.

"Wait." Lorelei holds up her hand. "You brought me to an axe-throwing place, where Xander also is, and you expect me not to throw said axe at *him*?"

"I said *be nice*," I reply. "And I suspect that Xander can handle himself."

Lorelei just snorts as Lucy waves us over to where she stands with the others.

"This is *so* fun," Lucy says. "Which one of you thought of this?"

"Not I," Jonas says with a laugh. "This is new to me."

"Giles thought of it," Xander adds. "And I agree. It should be fun."

"No killing each other," Lucy says, looking right at Lorelei, who just shrugs a shoulder.

"I make no promises."

"I hit the bullseye *three times*," Breena reminds us and takes a sip of her beer as we all sit in a pizza parlor, the kind with sawdust on the floor and paper plates.

"Cheers to that," Xander says, tapping his beer glass to hers. "You kicked ass, little one."

"I really did." Breena preens and reaches for a slice of the pie. "This was a really good idea. Throwing axes and picturing all the garbage we're dealing with as the target was really cathartic."

"We won't talk about how I almost killed Jonas," Lucy says, cringing as she looks at her husband. "I didn't know you were walking out there."

"You can't get rid of me that easily," he says and kisses her forehead.

"The aunts invited all of us over for dinner tomor-row," Lucy informs us as Lorelei fakes gagging at the public display of affection. "She invited Giles's parents, too. It should be fun."

"What do we need to bring?" Lorelei wants to know. "I forgot to ask my mom when she called."

"Nothing that I know of," Lucy replies. "I think they're having it catered."

"Hot. Holy Hades, this is hot." Breena fans her mouth with her hand. "Fresh from the oven."

"And so good," Lucy agrees.

"I could make a carrot cake," Breena says, thinking it over. "Wait. No, I can't. I'm planning to drink just a little too much tonight, and I don't have time to get it done before we go to their house tomorrow."

"I'm sure they have it covered," Lucy assures her.

"I won't be able to make it," Xander says as he stares down at his uneaten pizza.

"Why not?" Breena asks.

"I have some things to see to," he replies. "I'll call Astrid and Hilda in the morning and let them know."

"If you change your mind—" Breena begins, but Xander shakes his head.

"I won't."

I watch my friend as he goes through the motions of eating his dinner and smiling as the others make jokes, but I can see that something is off with him tonight.

I've known Xander for as long as I can remember. He's an intense man with a lot of responsibilities on his shoulders. But I've never seen him like *this*.

He turns his gaze to me and offers an almost imperceptible shake of the head as if to say: "*Don't worry. I'm fine.*"

I tip back my glass and drink the one beer I'm allowing myself tonight since I'm driving the girls home. However, I plan to have a long conversation with my friend before the day ends.

"I need to go over to Xander's." Breena and I just got home after dropping off Lorelei, and she looks up with concern.

"Is everything okay?"

"I don't know. That's why I need to go over there. I feel like something's off, and I want to ask him about it.

It didn't seem right to interrogate him in front of everyone when we were supposed to be having fun."

"That makes sense." She bites her lip and looks worried. "I wonder if *it* has been taunting him, too."

"I'll find out." I wrap my arms around her and kiss her softly. "Are you okay here by yourself?"

"Of course. I have Merlin." The lights flicker. "And Molly. I'm not alone."

"Okay. I shouldn't be long."

I kiss her once more and then set off for Xander's. He doesn't live far from me, but I decide to drive the short distance to his house anyway. It's just not worth taking any chances right now.

The porch light is on when I climb the steps, and the door swings open before I can even ring the bell.

"Did Breena call you?" I step inside and close the door behind me.

"No, I'm psychic," Xander replies with a rueful smile. "And you're my friend. You're worried about me."

"Yeah, as a matter of fact, I am. You've seemed off since we were at Breena's the other day. What happened over there, X?"

He blows out a breath, and when he drops onto the sofa and pushes his hands through his long, black hair, he just looks *exhausted*.

"We've seen some shit." He looks over at me. "We both know there's a lot out in the universe we can't explain, and we just accept it. We roll with it and chalk it up to the paranormal."

"Sure."

"What I saw in that place goes far beyond that." He leans forward, his elbows resting on his knees. He looks *scared.*

I've never seen Xander afraid of anything. To say it's unsettling is a vast understatement.

"And what was that, Xander?"

"It was absolute and utter destruction. It was our ruin and what happens after. I've understood from the beginning that this thing wants to kill witches. That it *enjoys* the hunt. And far too many of us have fallen to him. It's frustrating to know that I haven't been able to stop it."

He pauses and licks his lips.

"But?"

"But I don't know if I'm strong enough for what's required of us."

"You're the strongest person I know. Mentally, physically, and with your abilities."

"I'm not convinced it'll be enough." He shakes his head and stands to pace his living space, stopping by the windows. He stares outside, his hands in his pockets, and rocks back on his heels. "I watched it kill Lorelei. It was as plain as day. It showed me everything it has planned for her, and then it laughed with so much joy and glee it made me want to throw up."

"It's been taunting all of us for days, X. This is what it wants, for us to be afraid and unsure. To second-guess ourselves."

"Of course, I'm fucking second-guessing myself." He whirls to me, rage and fear radiating off him in waves. "I love her more than life itself. My survival depends on hers because if anything ever happened to her, I'd die of a broken heart on the spot."

"But you won't tell *her* that."

"She doesn't want to hear it. Besides, she already knows." He waves that aside. "It doesn't matter how she feels about it, it's still the truth. And I know it's going to try to kill her. The mere thought of that paralyzes me with so much fear, I don't know what to do about it."

"Shake it off."

He stares at me with disgust. "What did you say?"

"Shake it the fuck off. It wants you scared. That's why it showed you what it did. Do you think it doesn't know what all our fears are? It's not human, X. Of course, it knows. And it's going to exploit them every chance it gets. It's playing with you, and right now, it's winning. You need to shrug off the fear and get damn pissed off instead because the fear is what that thing needs to win."

Xander goes quiet for a moment and then lets out a long breath, his shoulders sagging.

"You're right. You're absolutely right. I let it get inside my head and gave it exactly what it wanted."

"Because no matter how much you try to show us all otherwise, you *are* a human being. And you love her."

"She's everything." His black eyes meet mine. "You know how that feels."

I nod, thinking about Breena. "I do. There isn't anything I wouldn't do to make sure Breena's safe. And if it showed me what you saw, it would unnerve the hell out of me. Jesus, I saw a dead body sitting next to Lorelei in the back seat of my car on our way to Boston tonight, and I thought my soul was going to leave my body."

"You *what*?"

I shake my head and wave him off. "Calm down. It wasn't really there. It was in the mirror. This thing has decided that it's fun to fuck with us through reflections. But Lorelei saw it, too, and it scared her. Then, Breena basically told it to go fuck itself, and it did."

"*Breena* said that?"

"Yeah. She's fed up with the games this thing's been throwing around. So am I. The thing is, I don't know how to stop it."

"Maybe there's a way through the mirrors," he mutters as he paces the room. "A spell we can cast to trap it there and then destroy the mirror."

"That actually sounds like a good idea. What's the spell?"

"I don't know, but I know some people we can call to ask for help." He turns to me. "You're absolutely right. I'm done being scared. It got what it wanted, and now it's done. And it's going to suffer for it."

"You've never been a vindictive witch."

"It's fucking with Lorelei," he says simply. "With all the girls. Hell yeah, I'm feeling particularly vindictive.

We're going to get rid of this son of a bitch once and for all."

"Let's start researching."

"It's late," he replies.

"I'm here, and I have nowhere else to be. Let's get started."

"Okay."

CHAPTER FIFTEEN
BREENA

"I'm so glad you ladies were able to come early before everyone else arrives for dinner so we can work on Beltane preparations," my mom says as we all gather around the kitchen table. She has dried flowers spread out so we can make wreaths, flower crowns, and maypoles. Lucy brought fresh flowers for some of the same things and also for flower cones.

"I love spring," Polly, Giles's mom, says with a happy smile. "The flowers are just so *refreshing*. Winter always makes me sad."

"Oh, no," Lorelei says as she picks up a lilac. "This one is already starting to wilt."

Lucy wiggles her fingers and smiles at the bloom, plumping it right back up.

"Well, that's handy," Polly says with a laugh and then glances at the doorway. "Hello, Agatha."

Lucy's head whips over to the doorway. I can see

she's hoping to see her mother, but I can tell by the way her shoulders sag that she can't.

"If it makes you feel any better," I say to Lucy, "I can't see her either."

"It seems you and I are the only ones who can't," Lucy says with a pout. "I thought I'd get to see her regularly after last fall, but no. She's hiding from me again."

"Not hiding," Astrid says, shaking her head. "She just knows you don't need her right now."

"I always need her," Lucy whispers and then shudders. "Whoa, what was that?"

"She just put her hand on your shoulder," Lorelei tells Lucy. "And she kissed the top of your head. You may not be able to see her, but she's with you, and she loves you."

Lucy's eyes fill with tears, but she smiles at Lorelei. "Thanks. I needed that."

"I know," Lorelei says and then looks at her own mother. "If you ever do that to me, I'll be really, really mad at you."

Astrid laughs and stands to take care of the boiling water she has on the stove for tea. "Do we know what kind of activities are planned for the Beltane festival this year? Hilda and I decided not to be on the committee this time."

"There will be music," Polly begins, "and lots of food. Some ritual magic."

"Dancing naked under the moon?" I ask, and Polly nods her head.

"If you'd like to, of course."

"I was kidding," I reply, shaking my head.

"Well, going skyclad is completely optional," Astrid reminds me. "But you have a lovely figure, darling, and you should consider it. It's quite the liberating and spiritual experience."

"I think I'll pass, thanks." I laugh and reach for another bunch of tulips, but they're dead when I pull them to me. "Lucy, you need to work your magic on these."

I glance up, feeling like the wind has been knocked out of my lungs.

Everything in the room is *dead*. Not just the flowers but also the people. All of them are slumped over, their eyes wide and skin decaying in front of me. The stench of death and blood fills the air, making me gag.

"Stop it," I whisper. "This isn't real."

"Oh, darling, they're all with me now." Agatha catches my attention and grins at me in that horrible, sinister way I've come to absolutely despise. "Come along. Join us. It's so freeing to be on the other side. You don't have to be afraid."

"I'm not afraid. I'm pissed off, you son of a bitch."

Agatha's face crumples in rage. "You're *nothing*. Do you hear me? You're nothing, and you're going to die in the most painful way imaginable."

I stand and raise my hands at the apparition that isn't my aunt at all and speak loudly and with intent.

"You're not real. This is all a lie, and lies aren't

welcome here. Be gone." I slice my hand through the air and then continue with a spell.

"This is not your place, this is not your time, be gone from my sight at the end of this rhyme. Take your deceit, your torturous glee, return to your hell, so mote it be."

Agatha's face twists in pain, and then she disappears altogether.

"Darling, what's wrong?" I blink at my mother, who's watching me with concern.

"Huh?"

"What happened?" Polly asks. "Should I call Giles?"

"No." I shake my head and sit. "Sorry. *It* tried to scare me, but I got rid of it."

"How?" Mom demands.

"You were all dead." I swallow hard and then shrug it off. "But I knew it was a lie. You're not dead, and it's gone now."

"We need to figure out a way to get it gone for good," Lucy says.

"I think we've figured that out."

We glance at the door, surprised to see all the guys there, even Giles's dad.

"I didn't think you were coming today," Lorelei says to Xander, who just frowns at her.

"We came early because we wanted to run something by all of you," Giles says as he reaches for a cookie. "And I'm in luck with the cookies."

"Not too many," Astrid says, shaking a finger at him. "Dinner isn't far away."

Giles smiles at her and then nods at Jonas.

"The killer has been using mirrors to mess with everyone," Jonas begins. "It happened to Lucy and me in the shop this morning, and Giles tells me he and Breena have also been dealing with it of late."

"Yes," I confirm. "And Lorelei, too, in the car yesterday."

"Creepy as hell," Lorelei breathes out.

"We think there must be a spell we can work to trap it in a mirror and then destroy it," Xander says.

"Of course," I murmur. "Why on earth didn't we think of that sooner? It's so simple."

"But not easy," Astrid replies immediately, shaking her head. "I've never heard of such a spell working, Xander. Others have tried, but it's not just a reflection of what's happening, it's another dimension entirely. What you're suggesting means destroying that entire dimension."

"There's a way," Jonas replies, opening a Book of Shadows he was carrying. "And it would only destroy the dimension in that particular mirror, not the reality as a whole."

"Impossible," my mom mutters. "You're starting to dive into things you don't understand. We don't mess with the other side. We don't stick our noses into the multiverse. It can be catastrophic."

"What choice do we have?" Xander demands, anger radiating from him. Neither my mom nor Astrid looks surprised, and they don't back down from the big man.

But Lorelei slowly gets to her feet.

"I will not sit idly by as a *ghost* decides to taunt and torture the women I love," Xander continues. "And that's every single one of you and the others in the coven. I will do whatever it takes to destroy it and keep every single one of you safe."

"What you're talking about is dangerous," Astrid reminds him. "You, any of you, could end up trapped in an alternate reality, Xander."

"It's a chance I'm willing to take."

"No." I shake my head as I stand to pace the kitchen. "No, Xander. There has to be another way."

"If you discover it, I'm all ears," he replies, his face set in grim lines. "In the meantime, we'll be researching *this* way. I won't jump into anything without understanding all the ins and outs and ensuring we keep everyone safe."

"Including yourself," Lorelei says, speaking for the first time.

Xander doesn't reply.

"I said, including *yourself*, Xander." Lorelei crosses to him, going toe-to-toe with him. Seeing the short woman squaring off with a man close to seven feet tall, would be laughable, but she has pure anger in every line of her body. "You will not be the sacrificial lamb."

"You don't need to worry about it," is Xander's only response. The aunts and Polly all roll their eyes.

"Goddess save us from men and their masculinity," Polly mutters. "Lorelei's right, Xander. The only way to do this is if *every single one of you* is safe."

"You will *not* sacrifice yourself," Lorelei says to Xander. "I won't have it."

"I didn't ask," he replies. His voice is hard but not unkind.

Lorelei turns on her heel and walks out the door.

"I'll go," Astrid says, hurrying after her daughter.

"We aren't stupid," Giles assures us all. "A lot of planning and research will go into this before we do anything, but we have to do *something*. Otherwise, we're just sitting ducks, waiting for it to make its next move."

"We need to be on the offensive," Jonas says with a nod. "I think it's a good idea. I wish I had access to my coven in Hallows End. They might know what to do."

"But you can't ask them," I guess, and he nods grimly.

"It's okay. There are others we can ask, both locally and all over the country." Lucy looks at me and then at Lorelei. "I know we called Miss Sophia before, but she might be able to help us with this, too."

"She's out of the country," Polly informs her with a frown. "She and her granddaughter are on a trip to Ireland."

"Wow, good for them," Lucy says. "I'll still send her a note so she can get back to me when she returns. And I'll reach out to the other witches in New Orleans. They're really smart people, and they've been through a hell all their own."

"Good idea." Xander nods. "I'm going to call my father."

We all go still, sure we misheard him.

"I'm sorry, what?" I finally ask.

"You heard me," he replies. "He's an asshole, but he's a powerful witch. He might have answers."

"Do you even know where he is?" I ask him. Xander hasn't seen his father since he was a little boy.

"I know," Xander says with a nod and glances at the door Lorelei left through. "I'm going to go call him. I'll keep you all posted on what I find out."

"Won't you stay for dinner?" Mom asks. "You can deal with your father later once you've had something to eat."

"Thank you, Hilda, but I'd like to get this over with. You all enjoy."

He nods and walks out, and I look over at Giles. "Are you sure about this?"

"Nope. But it's the only thing we have right now, so we're going to work through it."

I have a bad feeling about this.

"**H**ave you heard anything from Xander?" Giles and I are doing dishes, and it's been a full twenty-four hours since everything happened at my mom and Astrid's house. "I've been thinking about him all day and haven't heard a word."

"I haven't either," Giles says as he rinses a bowl and

places it in the dishwasher. "I tried to call him earlier, but there was no answer."

"That's not like him."

"I'll give him until tomorrow morning, and then I'll just show up at his house," he replies. "Will you pass me that salad bowl?"

"Sure." I hand it over and then return to scrubbing the pan I used to sauté the chicken. "Have you had anything weird happen today?"

"Not really. You?"

"No. And, honestly, that makes me nervous because I know *something* will happen eventually, and I wish it would just get it over with already."

Giles smiles over at me. "And here I always pegged you as an optimist."

"I am, but you have to admit, something usually happens every day."

"Just don't think about it."

I snort and then glance over to Merlin's food dish, frowning. "Merlin hasn't eaten anything today."

"Must not be hungry."

I glance around but don't see the cat anywhere in the kitchen. "He almost always empties his bowl by this time of the day. You know, I don't remember seeing him earlier when I was working at my altar, and Merlin *loves* altar work."

"Maybe he got trapped in a room. He's always running in and out of places. I might have accidentally closed him in the pantry when I was making dinner," Giles suggests and walks over to the pantry, but when he opens the door and peers inside, he shakes his head. "Not in there."

"I'm going to check around the house." I wipe my hands on a towel and walk toward the sunroom. "Merlin? Where are you, baby?"

He's not in the sunroom. And after a few frantic moments of both Giles and me checking the entire ground floor, we come up empty.

"You check outside," I suggest as I head for the stairs. "I'll go upstairs."

"On it," Giles says, headed for the back door.

"Merlin," I call out as I ascend the stairs. "If you're being lazy somewhere and ignoring us, I'm going to be mad. It's not funny."

I check the bedrooms, my tapestry room, and the bathrooms. Sometimes, Merlin likes to nap in the sink.

But he's not there.

"Any luck?" Giles calls up the stairs.

"No." I stand at the top of the stairs, my hands on my hips. "I take it you didn't find him."

He shakes his head. "Where would he go?"

Worry starts to settle in my stomach as my cell rings in my pocket. "Hey, Lucy. You haven't seen Merlin by any chance, have you? I know it's a weird question, but—"

"He's right here," Lucy replies. "I found him out on the porch, sunning himself. When I opened the door, he just waltzed right in as if he owned the place. Nera was happy to see him."

I frown and then shrug. "Weird. Okay, I'll come and get him. Thanks, Luce."

"Sure thing. No rush. He's fine here."

"Okay, see you soon." I hang up and walk down the steps to Giles. "He's at Lucy's. I have no idea how he got out or why he went to her place, but at least he's safe and sound. I'll run over and grab him."

"I'll come with you."

"You don't have to." I can see how tired he is. Giles has been working full time while also dealing with the stress of a paranormal maniac trying to kill us all. "I won't be long, and then I'll come back, and we can curl up and watch a movie or something."

He narrows his eyes on me. "Are you sure? Because I don't mind."

"You're exhausted."

He blows out a breath and tips his forehead to mine. "Yeah, I am. But you're more important."

"I'm *fine*. Honest. It won't take me long, and I'll be perfectly safe. Lucy and Jonas are on the other side of this little adventure, and you're here."

"Okay." He kisses my forehead and walks me to the door. "Go get your familiar. I'm going to have a little chat with him when he gets home. He doesn't need to be pulling shit like this."

"He's a cat," I remind him with a laugh. "But sure, you go ahead and have that talk. I'll see you in a few."

I blow Giles a kiss and then get in my car and head for Lucy's apothecary. She lives and works in the same building, and it's one of my favorite spots in town. Her gardens are *amazing*, which is pretty standard for a green witch, and everything she offers in her shop is full of magic.

I might have to do a little shopping while I'm there.

She's already flipped the *Closed* sign on the door when I arrive, so I walk around to the back door, which is where Lucy and Jonas come and go from. I peek inside and see Lucy at the stove. She waves me inside.

"Hey," I say as I walk in and spot Merlin lying on the floor next to Nera. "So, you just decided to visit your old pal here?"

Merlin just blinks those big eyes at me and doesn't move.

"What a stinker." I shake my head and turn to Lucy. "What are you making?"

"Jonas's favorite. Fish and chips."

"Yum. I didn't know that was his favorite. I didn't realize they had fish and chips in colonial America."

"They didn't," Lucy says with a laugh. "This is a new favorite."

"Ah, I see. How was your day?"

"Really good, actually," she tells me. "It was just a *normal* day, and I'm not going to question or complain about it."

"Same here." I pluck a grape off a bunch in a fruit

bowl and pop it into my mouth. "Just a regular, run-of-the-mill day. It was kind of nice."

Lucy pauses and looks over at me. "Why do I feel like it's the calm before the storm?"

I shrug as she turns back to the stove, and I reach for another grape. "Well, it very well might be, but in the meantime, I'm going to enjoy it. Where is Jonas, anyway?"

"He's in Hallows End," Lucy says, reaching for another potato to cut into french fries. "He goes every day around this time to check on things. So far, everything's been normal over there, so that's good."

"Yeah, one less thing for Jonas to worry about." I eat another grape. "I just ate not long ago, but these grapes are delicious. So sweet."

Lucy glances over and then frowns. "Those aren't grapes. They're flowers."

"Whatever. I know what grapes taste like, and these are grap—" I look down at my hand and see that I'm not holding a grape but a lilac flower. "What in the world? They were grapes three seconds ago."

"No, I don't have any grapes in the house. And I never keep fruit on the table. It's always a bowl of flowers. You know that."

I blink up at her, but I don't understand. "What?"

"Well, it *was* a normal day. Breena, are you okay?"

"Sure. Of course, I am." I lower myself into a kitchen chair and pluck at my lips. "I'm numb. I can't feel my face."

"Damn it, Breena. Did you only eat the lilacs? That wisteria is poisonous."

"Wisteria?" My stomach starts to lurch, and I know I'm in trouble. "Oh, no."

"Yeah, oh, no. Come on, let's go throw up."

Lucy takes my hand and helps me into the bathroom. I hug the toilet as all of today's food comes back up.

I can hear Lucy talking behind me, but I can't make out the words. I feel dizzy and disoriented.

"Ambulance is coming," she says into my ear. "On the phone with poison control. Damn it, Breena, don't you black out on me. This plant won't kill you, but it will make you really uncomfortable for a while. I need you to drink some water."

I shake my head. I'm dizzy, and I feel sick. My mouth burns. I just want to go home, and I want Giles.

Where is Giles?

"Giles."

"I'll call him, but first, you need to drink this water. It'll help."

"No." I shake my head again, or at least I think I do, but she's still holding the glass to my lips. I take a little sip, and it burns my mouth, making me cry out.

"Oh, honey, I'm so sorry." Lucy kisses my forehead. "I hear the ambulance. We'll get you to the hospital, and they can help you."

"So sick. Hurts."

"I know. I know. And I'm so sorry. In here!" I hear people running and Lucy talking, and then I'm on a gurney, being wheeled out to the ambulance. I see Jonas come running up, his face ashen and full of concern as he reaches Lucy, who's talking to him, likely telling him what happened.

"I'd like to come with you," Jonas says to the EMT. With a nod of permission, Jonas jumps in next to me. "Lucy is calling Giles now. I'll stay with you."

"Thank you." I reach for his hand and hold on tightly. "Scared."

"I'm sure you are, beautiful girl. You're going to be fine. We'll get this all taken care of."

We're already moving quickly through town. The hospital isn't far from Lucy's house, and it only takes what seems like seconds before we're pulling into the emergency bay.

More moving and people shouting. Jonas explains what happened to the doctor since I can't talk and am still so disoriented.

"Giles," I whisper and then see Lucy come into the room. "Giles?"

"I can't get him to answer the phone," she says, but she pastes a smile on her face. It doesn't matter, panic still sets in, and I flail about until someone has to forcibly hold me down. "Stop that, Breena. He's probably just in the shower or something. Xander is on his way to get him."

Tears leak from my eyes and run down my cheeks. I'm so uncomfortable, I want to climb out of my skin. Everything burns. Everything's spinning. I'm nauseous and suddenly feel like I'm going to crap my pants.

And now, no one can find Giles. What if he's in danger?

"Breena, we need you to calm down." The voice doesn't come from the doctor. It's coming from inside my head.

I look over and see Jonas looking at me intently. He nods.

"Yes, it's me. We need you to calm down, my darling. We can't help you until you calm down. Don't worry, Giles is just fine. Everything is going to be fine."

I feel more tears falling down my cheeks, but I take a deep breath and let it out again.

"Good. Very good. More breaths, just like that."

With Jonas talking to me in my head, I find my calm, and the doctor and nurses are able to get an IV started. It helps alleviate some of the horrible symptoms relatively quickly.

But I'm still so scared.

"Giles," I whisper.

"We'll find him," Lucy says, her hand on my leg. "He'll be here soon. I wouldn't lie to you about that."

I nod. No, she wouldn't. But what if something horrible happened to him? Why did I leave the house without him?

What if he's gone, and it's all my fault?

"You're panicking again," Jonas says in my head.

"*Slow, easy breaths, Breena. There's no need to be so anxious.*"

I nod and breathe with him, watching him. Jonas has quickly become one of my favorite people in the whole world, and I trust him implicitly.

He's like a brother to me.

He wouldn't lie.

"Good," Lucy says. "Very good. Are you starting to feel better?"

The nausea is almost gone, but my mouth still feels like it's on fire. "A little."

"It's going to take a few hours," the doctor says. I don't remember his name. "We'll keep her here until I'm sure all the symptoms are under control and the poison is out of her system."

"Thank you," Lucy says to him. "Thank you so much."

He nods, gives the nurse some orders, and then hurries out of my room and on to the next.

"Any word from Xander?" I ask.

"You're speaking in full sentences," Lucy says with a grin. "You *are* feeling better. Not yet, but he'll probably bring Giles straight here."

"I hope so." I lean my head back and close my eyes. "Goddess, I hope so."

Breena! I need you, baby.

I frown at the sound of Giles's voice in my head.

"What's happening?"

CHAPTER SIXTEEN
GILES

"She'll be fine," I assure myself as I wander into the living room and sit on the sofa. The book I've been reading about a sapphire mine in Montana sits on the end table, so I pick it up, lie back on the couch, and open it up to where I left off the last time I read it.

The Yogo mine is in the mountains of central Montana, and they recently reopened it for digging, which is really exciting. It's a bucket list trip for me to go and tour the area.

Just as I flip a page, Merlin jumps up onto my stomach and starts to make biscuits, purring loudly.

"What in the hell?" I narrow my eyes on him. "Where were you? I thought you were at Lucy's."

I start to call out for Breena, thinking maybe she's back already, but my phone pings with a text.

Breena: *Hey! Gonna hang out here and chat with Lucy for a while. Just letting you know.*

I grin and send back a heart, then settle in with the cat. "I guess it's you and me for a little bit. I can't believe you were hiding from us the whole time."

Merlin purrs contentedly, and I go back to my book, but not long after, my eyes feel heavy. Breena wasn't wrong when she said I looked exhausted. I am. I've been busy at Gems, and the mental toll this whole thing has taken on me is significant.

So, when my eyes close and I feel sleep bearing down on me, I don't fight it. Maybe what I need until Breena comes home is a little nap.

"There is no time to write anything down, Giles. We must go now."

"I do not want to write anything down. I need to destroy the book. If they find it, they will surely execute us, Martha."

"They will do so anyway. Come, make haste. We must run. Leave everything."

I should have taken Martha out of here months ago. We should have loaded up the wagon and gone to my children in Boston, but I never dreamed the hysteria would spread so far and so quickly.

Or that so many would die.

"Giles Corey, come out of your home immediately."

Martha and I freeze and stare at each other in horror.

"No," she says, already weeping. "No, Giles."

"'Tis nothing." I kiss her forehead. "They merely have inquiries, nothing more."

She only shakes her head as I walk away from her and out the front door. The sheriff, George Corwin, who should not hold that title at all and would not at his tender age of five and twenty if his uncles were not judges, stands with his band of deputies at his back.

"Giles Corey, you are being charged with witchcraft. What say you?"

I simply shake my head. "I do not wish to enter a plea."

George narrows his eyes. "You must."

I do not reply; I simply look down at the ground. "No, sir."

"Take him," George orders. I am flanked on either side by two men, each taking one of my frail arms as they carry me to a wagon.

I look back and see Martha standing in our doorway, weeping as she watches them take me away. Is this the last time I shall see her lovely face? Will they take me straight to the gallows?

Instead, I am led directly into a courtroom, and Thomas Newton, the prosecutor, stands before the judges, ready for my trial.

I do not have a solicitor.

"Giles Corey," the judge begins, "you are formally charged with being a witch. What say you?"

"I will not enter a plea." I firm my jaw as the room quiets in surprise.

"You must enter a plea so we may move forward with these proceedings," the judge replies.

"I will not."

"You refuse?"

"I do, sir."

The judge watches me and rubs his hand over his mouth, then points to George, who is standing in the back of the courtroom.

"Sheriff, take Mister Corey out and press him until he enters a plea."

My heart stops. Surely, I must have misheard. Perhaps this is a bluff to get me to enter a plea.

My arms are seized again, and they drag me into the middle of the street, where a crowd has already begun to gather 'round.

"On the ground," George orders, and I am unceremoniously thrown down. My poor back aches from the fall.

They place a door over me, and it already makes it hard to breathe.

"Before we add the first boulder, Giles Corey, what say you in regards to the charge of witchcraft?"

They cannot do this. It has to be a ruse.

"Weight," I call out. There is a loud whack, *and then it is even harder to breathe.*

I remain there for three days. Sometimes, I pass out and can escape the agony. But then I awaken again and am thrust into the middle of a nightmare.

I feel death growing close. But, honestly, it will be a welcome reprieve from the pain.

BANG! BANG! BANG!

"Giles, open up!"

I gasp for air and tug on my shirt, pulling it away from my chest. It feels too tight. Goddess, I can't fucking *breathe.*

"Giles, open the door!"

"Lorelei?" I push Merlin off my stomach and stand, then stumble to the door and yank it open.

Lorelei's eyes widen. "What in the name of Freya is going on here? You look like...I don't even know."

"Nightmare." I continue to gasp for breath. "Fucking nightmare. I was Giles in 1692, and I was being crushed."

"Holy shit," she mutters and frames my face with her cool hands. "Breathe. You're in modern-day Salem, and no one is killing you, Giles. You're safe."

I nod and take a long, deep breath.

"Thanks. I'm okay. What's wrong? Why are you here?"

"Lucy called me and said Breena passed out on her back porch. We need to get over there."

I scowl. "That doesn't make sense. Breena texted me and told me she was visiting with Lucy."

"My guess is *she didn't* text you."

I reach for my phone and check. Sure enough, there is no text from Breena.

But there are several missed calls from Lucy.

"For fuck's sake," I mutter and hurry out the door after Lorelei. "She went over there to find Merlin, but not long after she left, the damn cat jumped up onto the couch with me."

"This is so fucking weird," Lorelei grumbles as we drive to Lucy's house. "And today had been such a nice, normal day, too. Literally *nothing* out of the ordinary happened, and I was enjoying the hell out of it."

"It gave us a false sense of security." I drag my hand down my face, trying not to freak out at the thought of Breena passed out at Lucy's house while I slept on the couch with a purring cat.

It's absolutely fucking unacceptable.

"We have to do something about this son of a bitch," Lorelei says. "I'm sick to death of being his play toy. Of *all of us* being his play toys. Who the hell does he think he is, anyway?"

"He thinks he can do whatever he wants. Kill whomever he wants. We *are* his toys, Lorelei, and he'll keep doing this bullshit until we stop him."

She doesn't reply as we hurry the short distance to Lucy's. When she parks, I rush out of the car and up the steps to the house.

"What's going on?" I demand as soon as I see Jonas standing by the back door.

"I wasn't here," Jonas replies, holding up his hands. "I was in Hallows End when it happened. Lucy is in the guest room, where Breena's lying down."

I rush past him and up the steps to the second floor, finding the two women in the guest room, as Jonas said.

Lucy pats Breena's forehead with a wet cloth, and Breena looks so pale it makes my heart ache.

"See? He's right here," Lucy says, pointing to me.

"Giles!" Breena sits up and reaches for me. I pull her into my arms. She clings to me as if she thought she'd never see me again. "Oh, my goddess, I thought something horrible happened to you."

"Hey, I'm fine, baby. I'm right here. I'm not going anywhere." I rock her back and forth and look up at Lucy, who's pale and looks like she might be sick. I wink at her, and she tries to offer me a smile, but I can tell it's forced. I tip Breena's face up so I can look at her. "I think you've given everyone a scare, sweetheart."

"Scared me, that's for sure," Lucy says, trying to keep her voice light. "And I don't think it's something I'd like to go through again. Twice is enough for me."

"Twice?" Breena asks.

"Yeah, once during Samhain last year and then again today. Sure, this was less dramatic, but it was no less scary."

"What happened, exactly?" Lorelei demands as she climbs onto the opposite side of the bed from me and takes Breena's hand. "And don't leave anything out. I want to know everything."

"Merlin came to Lucy's house earlier today," Breena begins and swallows hard. "Giles and I couldn't find him at the house, and we looked everywhere. But then Lucy called to tell me he was here, so I came over to get him. Lucy and I were chatting while she made fish and chips for Jonas, and I started eating grapes from a bowl on the table. They were *so* good, I couldn't stop eating them, but they weren't grapes. They were poisonous flowers, and I got violently sick. My mouth burned, and I couldn't stop throwing up. I was dizzy and just so nauseous I couldn't stand it. The ambulance came and took me to the hospital. Jonas rode with me in the ambulance. Then, when we were in the room at the hospital, and I was freaking out because no one could find Giles for me, Jonas was talking to me in my head to help calm me down."

She looks around the room, likely seeking out Jonas, and finds him standing in the doorway. She offers him a sweet smile.

"You were the only thing that could keep me calm. Gosh, I love you, Jonas."

"I love you, too, precious one." He smiles gently. "What else do you remember?"

"I just wanted Giles, but no one could find him. Lucy said that Xander went to get him, but they never came to the hospital, and it felt like we were waiting forever for them. And then I heard Giles in my head, calling out for me, telling me he needed me. Then everything changed, and I was in *this* bed, not the hospital bed. But Lucy and Jonas were still here. I'm so confused."

"Okay." I pull her against me again and pat her back soothingly. "Why don't you tell us what you saw, Lucy?"

"Well, Breena just showed up out of the blue at my

back door. I was happy to see her and waved her in, but she didn't come inside. She just passed out right there on the porch. Jonas was just coming back from Hallows End, and he brought her up here. I tried to call you, Giles, but you didn't answer, so I called Lorelei, and she offered to swing by and get you. And she did."

"But you called to tell me to come get Merlin," Breena says to Lucy, who's already shaking her head.

"Actually, just after you left, Merlin hopped onto the couch with me," I tell Breena, frowning. "And when I was about to call out to see if you were already home, you texted me and told me you were going to stay and chat with Lucy for a while."

"But I didn't—"

"I know," I continue. "I realize now that you didn't text me at all. After Merlin curled up with me on the couch, I fell asleep and had a doozy of a nightmare. I woke up when Lorelei banged on the door to get me."

"He looked really shaken," Lorelei adds. "The only time I've ever seen him look that bad was when everything went down last year. His eyes looked so haunted."

"Did you have a nightmare?" Jonas asks.

As I remember it, I let out a shaky breath and tell them about it. "Yes, you could call it that. I was being pressed to death, as Giles Corey, in 1692."

"So much for our normal day," Lucy says grimly. "That sounds like a pretty shitty dream to me."

"It wasn't fun," I agree. "And it all just felt so *real*. That's the second time I've had that vision of Giles. This is the first time I was actually the man himself, though, and not just a spectator."

"I wonder if *it* plans to try to kill you that same way," Lorelei ponders out loud. "Like he's trying to show you: *This is how I plan to make you suffer.*"

"Isn't that a lovely thought?" Lucy asks, sarcasm dripping from every word. "For the goddess's sake, Lorelei."

"What?" Lorelei holds up her hands. "Nothing about this is lovely. We have to consider that possibility."

"As unpleasant as it is," Jonas adds, "she could be right."

"That is *not* how I plan to go out," I say. "No way."

"None of us is dying at the hands of that *thing*," Lorelei says.

"I wasn't poisoned?" Breena asks, wiping away her tears. "I didn't eat wisteria?"

"No," Lucy replies, shaking her head again. "I don't even have wisteria in the house. You didn't eat anything, I promise."

"But you were talking to me," Breena says, looking at Jonas.

"I was trying to reach you while you were unconscious," he confirms. "I know you're not clairvoyant, but sometimes when a person is under, it's easier to reach them telepathically. It sounds to me like you might have heard me."

"I think so," Breena replies softly. "Your voice was so reassuring. Thank you for that."

"Of course." Jonas wraps his arm around his wife and smiles down at Breena.

"Ugh. I want to go home." Breena fights tears again. "I'm so sorry this happened."

"Please don't apologize for something that isn't your fault," Lucy says and then frowns. "You know, I never did hear back from Xander. I called him and left a message, but he hasn't replied at all."

"I haven't heard from him today either," I add.

"If he had to deal with his father, he's probably in hermit mode," Lorelei says. "He has big feelings to deal with when it comes to his parents. He might just be licking some emotional wounds."

"Maybe you should go check on him," Breena suggests to Lorelei, who looks mildly taken aback at the thought. "You know him best, Lora. Maybe he needs someone to talk to."

"Yeah, well, I'm not that person for Xander anymore. He made damn sure of that." Lorelei stands up from the bed and walks to the door. "I'm glad everything's okay here. Let me know if you need anything else. I'll be at home, trying to write, but I'll keep my phone nearby."

And with that, she walks past Jonas, and we hear her descend the stairs.

"She's so stubborn," Lucy mutters. "But no one can make her figure her shit out when it comes to Xander. She has to do that on her own."

"She may never figure it out," Breena says softly. "I don't know exactly what went down there, but it broke something in her. And even though we all know they're fated, I'm afraid they'll never find their way back to each other and will both end up alone."

"I'd say it broke a piece of him, as well." I kiss Breena's head and then offer her my hand. "Come on, let's get you home. Do you feel well enough to walk?"

"I think so." She takes my hand and stands. "Yeah, I'm fine. Much better than I felt a few minutes ago. You said Merlin is at home?"

"He is."

"Well, good. What a weird evening."

"You're not kidding," Lucy says. "But I'm glad I saw you pass out so I could help you right away."

"Me, too." Breena hugs her cousin close. "Thank you."

"I'd like to drive past Xander's house," I say to Breena as I steer her car through town. "We won't stop. I just want to see if the lights are on."

"Good idea. Let's stalk him."

I glance over at her and laugh, relieved that she sounds more like herself. "If the lights are on, I'll know he's home and just taking some time for himself."

"And if the house is dark?"

"Then he could be anywhere, and I'll be more worried."

"Well, then, I think we should drive by." She reaches

for my hand and presses it to her cheek. "I'm sure he's fine. I mean, he's *Xander.*"

"Even Xander is human."

"Of course, he is. But he's also always been a loner. Sure, he has the coven and all of us, but Xander isn't one to seek out help from others. I'm positive he's absolutely fine."

I turn onto his street. When we drive past his house, I see lights on upstairs, and I let out a breath of relief. Breena's right. He really is just taking some time for himself.

"See? He's there," Breena says. "Thank goodness. Now, you can stop worrying."

"I'll come by and see him in the morning. In the meantime, let's get you home. Do you need anything?"

"A shower," she decides. "I think I was sweating when I was freaked out. I want to wash all of that away."

"We can definitely arrange for that."

I pull into the driveway, and we walk into the house where Merlin is lazily picking away at his bowl of food.

"There you are." Breena picks him up mid-chew, much to the cat's dismay. "You scared me and got us all into some trouble. But that's not your fault. Oh, baby, are you okay?"

She buries her face in the cat's black fur and hugs him tightly.

Merlin looks annoyed.

"Meow."

"I know you don't love to be held, but I just need to for a minute." When she finally sets him down, Merlin returns to his food dish. "Okay, I really need that shower now. I'm going to use yours if that's okay with you. It's bigger."

"Excellent idea." I grin and lead Breena upstairs to the en suite bathroom in my bedroom and start the water for her as she fetches her shampoo and soap from the other bathroom.

"Maybe I should just keep this in both rooms so I don't have to carry it back and forth. Man, that is such a first-world statement to make."

"Personally, I think you should just move into this bathroom. Like I said before, I can take the other one."

"Hmm." She slips her shirt over her head and then boosts up onto her tiptoes to kiss me. "I'll think about it."

"And you guys accuse Lorelei of being stubborn. I'd say it runs in the family."

But then, all thoughts escape my mind entirely when Breena strips out of the rest of her clothes, not shy in the least to be standing naked in front of me, and then pulls her long, blonde hair up into a knot on the top of her head.

The gods knew what they were doing when they made Breena. Her body is soft and smooth with curvy hips and breasts. Her stomach isn't flat, and I love it. She's strong and just flat-out beautiful.

"You're staring at my fat stomach," she says, scowling

at me. "I would prefer if you'd ogle my boobs. They're better."

"Every bit of you is perfect."

I tug my shirt over my head, step out of my jeans, and follow Breena into the shower.

"Oh, this is a party for two?" she asks with a grin.

"You can't just strip naked in front of me, look as smokin' hot as you do, and then expect me to walk the other way. That's not how this works."

"That's good to know." She grins and boldly wraps her hand around my cock. "Because I had a feeling I'd be lonely in here all by myself. It might be why I chose the bigger shower."

"How convenient."

I reach down and grip the backs of her thighs, then easily lift her and brace her back against the tile.

"Whoa! That's cold."

I smile against her lips. "It'll warm up."

"I hope so."

Chapter Seventeen
Breena

I forget all about the cold tile when Giles slips inside me, his eyes pinned to mine, only stopping when he's balls-deep. He's breathing hard, and every muscle is pulled tight.

"Never, not once in my life, has it ever been like this." His voice is rough with lust and need and even a little awe.

"Oh, absolutely the same goes." I squeeze around him, and he leans in to bite my collarbone. "You just...*fit.*"

He hisses when I move again, and then he thrusts, in and out, as if he can't hold back any longer.

And I *love* that. I don't want him to be restrained. I want all of him, every time. I'm so greedy for it now, I can hardly stand it. When we were first together, I was shy and unsure, but now, I'm practically wanton.

It's fascinating.

And a *lot* of fun.

"Love this," I mutter as the whole room fills with steam. He's pounding into me now like a man possessed, and then he's suddenly coming apart. I watch without any feeling of self-consciousness.

And when he catches his breath and lifts his head from my shoulder, I can see all the love he has for me written all over his face.

It might be the sexiest part of all.

"Well, we didn't get clean, but we had a good time."

He laughs and slowly lowers me to my feet. "We'll get to the clean part now. Tip your head back. I'll wash your hair."

"You will? That's actually really sweet. There's nothing better than someone else scrubbing your scalp."

I do as he asks and let myself relax as Giles lathers up the shampoo in my hair. I reach out and grab his hips to keep myself steady. When he has the shampoo rinsed, he goes for the conditioner, and as that sits for a minute, the man gives me an honest-to-goddess scalp massage.

"Where did you learn this?" My voice is soft, and my eyes are closed as his fingers work their magic on my head.

"I have no idea. I just hope I'm doing it right."

"Feels pretty right to me." A door slams down the hall. "Molly would also like a massage."

"Yeah, well, Molly's out of luck. She'll have to find a ghost boyfriend to give her one."

I smirk, and then my eyes spring open when the bathroom door slams shut.

"She's really worked up over something."

"She gets this way sometimes," Giles replies. "She'll get over it. Let's rinse this out."

"Would you like me to wash *your* hair?"

"No thanks." He kisses me on the nose and then swats my butt playfully. "But thanks for the offer. I'd like to cuddle up on the sofa with a glass of wine and a movie."

"Oh, that sounds really good. A funny movie, though. I think we need to laugh."

"I'm on board with that. You choose."

Giles steps under the stream of water to quickly wash his hair as I pause getting out of the stall to watch him.

He's just so...*Giles.*

"How do you keep all those muscles so toned? I don't notice you going to the gym."

His eyes are tightly closed as he rinses his hair. "I carry heavy rocks around all day. And...genetics. I'm glad you like the looks of me."

"It's embarrassing, really, the way I pined away for you all those years. You were the sexiest thing I'd ever seen."

"Past tense?" He opens one eye.

"Now you're just fishing for compliments, and I'll make your head big, so I'll shut up now and get out of this shower."

Before I can leave, he snags me around the waist and pulls me against him.

"You're the sexiest woman I've ever seen in my life. Not only are you flat-out beautiful with those big green eyes and pretty hair and a killer smile, but your heart is absolutely gorgeous, too. You're sweet and kind, and you just want everyone around you to be happy. All of that together is sexy perfection."

"I wasn't fishing for a compliment," I whisper, but he just kisses me lightly. "But I'll take it. Thank you."

"Come on. Now that we've established how attractive we are, we should go watch that movie."

I step out of the shower first and reach for a towel.

"What in the hell?"

I whirl at the sound of Giles's voice. "What? What's wrong?"

He just points at the mirror and the message written on the foggy glass.

DANGER!

CRYSTAL BAD

HURTING US ALL

-M

Giles and I share a look, and then I hurry to dry myself off and reach for my clothes. Giles does the same.

"What in the heck?" I ask, hopping on one leg to get my pants on. "Has Molly ever left you messages on the glass before?"

"No." He pulls his shirt over his head. "I don't even

know if this is really her. For all we know, it could be *it* playing more games with us."

A door slams, and the lights flicker.

"I think it's Molly," I reply. "But I've been wrong before."

Giles opens the bathroom door, and Merlin darts from under the bed, straight at me, then jumps into my arms.

"He's shaking."

Giles looks grim as he watches me for a moment. "I think we have to give her the benefit of the doubt."

"I agree. What crystal is she talking about? You have hundreds of stones in this house."

He shakes his head but then realization seems to dawn in his eyes. "The labradorite that I brought home from the shop. I'll bet you anything that's the one. When it was at Gems, I had all those issues with poltergeist activity. Then I brought it home, and it stopped."

"What do we do?" I clutch a still-shaking Merlin to my chest and kiss his head.

"We destroy it." Giles's jaw is set as he sets off down the stairs. I hurry after him, still damp, my hair wet.

"Here, honey." I set Merlin on the sofa long enough to pull a hair tie out of my pocket and secure my wet locks in a bun and out of the way. As soon as I'm done, my familiar launches himself back into my arms. "He's a little clingy."

"Put him in his carrier and bring him with you,"

Giles suggests as he walks right for the big piece of crystal that sits on a stand in the living room.

"What are you going to do?"

"Smash it into a billion pieces." The stone flashes, startling me.

"Did you see that?"

"I saw. Labradorite is flashy, but not on its own like that. This is the issue. We're going to take away this bastard's conduit for its energy."

I urge Merlin into his crate and then carry him out into the yard with me, setting him where he can see me but far enough away that he won't get hurt.

"Should we call the others?" I ask.

"No. No time. I can do this." Giles pulls out a big, blue tarp and spreads it over the grass, setting the stone in the middle. Then, he walks to the shed and returns with two sledgehammers.

"You just keep those lying around?"

He grins. "Handily enough, yes. I'm going to break it first, and then together, we'll smash the smaller pieces. Then, we'll gather up the shards, separate it, and bury it."

"More burying," I murmur. "Okay, let's do it. We can get out some aggression by killing this thing."

"That's exactly what we're going to do. Kill this son of a bastard." Giles raises the hammer over his head and then smashes it down on the crystal, shattering it into several pieces.

There's a sharp scream, and blue light comes up out of the stone. Giles and I both jump back and watch as that scream fades and the light climbs into the sky and then dissipates.

"Are you kidding me?" I didn't realize I spoke out loud, but Giles's gaze whips to mine. "It was that simple the whole time?"

"It needed a power source and a place to hide. Now, that's all gone. I think it *was* that simple."

I advance on the stone, and together, Giles and I smash it into tiny pieces, then separate it into little piles, filling cheesecloth bags with the remnants.

"We have to bury these in different places," he says grimly. "And we don't really have time to get permission."

"We'll do it on public land or in the woods. It's dark, and we can do it quickly."

Giles raises an eyebrow. "I never pegged you as the type to be okay with doing something illegal."

"Is it illegal to bury crystals in this state? We're returning them to the earth, that's all."

"I really love you." He smiles proudly. "Come on. Let's do this."

"I have to put Merlin inside."

I take the cat indoors and open the crate. He comes out right away and sniffs the air. His back twitches, but then he curls up into a ball and begins taking a bath.

"I think he just gave us the all-clear."

"I can't sleep." I whisper it to Giles as we face each other in the bed, resting our cheeks on the pillows but looking at each other. "But I'm so tired. It was a crazy evening."

"What are you thinking about?" He reaches out and brushes my hair off my cheek.

"What do you think?"

He chuckles softly. "I know. My mind is going a mile a minute, too."

"How was it that easy? What if it's not really gone, and this was only more games? Not to mention, we just destroyed a crystal that's been in your family for more than three hundred years. That's heartbreaking."

"At the end of the day, it was just a rock, Breena."

"You don't believe that."

He lets out a breath. "It's true. I think there is great power in crystals. No, I *know* it. They are a conduit for energy, and they can heal. They can comfort. They can inspire love, productivity, and provide protection. But because they absorb energy, and because that particular stone has been in my family for so long, it makes sense that *it* used the stone to get to us. Labradorite is so powerful. It actually raises consciousness and grounds the spirit, which is exactly what *it* needed. Now that's gone. And if you think I won't burn the entire world to the ground if that's what it takes to keep you safe, you don't know me very well."

"I know you would. I know it. Have you noticed that even Molly has been quiet since we got home?"

He pauses and seems to listen. "You're right. Maybe we're all in recovery mode tonight."

"I've never dug so many holes in my life." I shift and pull the covers higher, tucking them under my chin. "Also, I should probably feel a little guilty that we buried some right next to Henry Thoreau's cabin at Walden Pond, but I'm not sorry."

"The best part was getting to check you for ticks when we got home." He waggles his eyebrows, making me giggle. "Henry might have gotten a kick out of it in his day."

"I wonder if Jonas ever met him," I say, thinking it over. "You know, at that time, Henry was good friends with Louisa May Alcott and Ralph Waldo Emerson. That was in the mid-eighteen hundreds. I wonder if Jonas knew of them then. He might have even walked past them on the street."

"Isn't that wild to think about?" Giles asks. "I mean, we know, logically, that Jonas has been on this Earth since the middle of the sixteen hundreds. But when you break it down like that and think of all the history he lived through, even just here in this little part of the world, it's mind-blowing. He was here when the minutemen were, during the Revolutionary War. It's really wild to think of everything he's seen."

"It almost hurts my brain when I do think about it,"

I admit. "And yet, despite all of that, he seems so...*normal.*"

"He could probably use some therapy, but no one would believe him," Giles replies. "I know I'd need to talk to someone if that happened to me."

"Maybe he talks to Lucy. I know it's not the same, but at least he has someone he can confide in now. For hundreds of years, he had to keep the secret to himself. That must have been torture."

"I can't imagine." He reaches over to gently drag his fingertips down my cheek. "If I didn't know better, I'd say you have a little crush on your cousin's husband."

I feel my cheeks flush, but I shake my head. "No, not in that way. Yes, Jonas is fascinating. He's always been so incredibly kind to me, and I know without a doubt that I can trust him. But the biggest thing that makes me love him?"

Giles lifts an eyebrow, waiting.

"How completely and utterly devoted he is to Lucy. Three hundred years separates them, but they immediately recognized each other, and he just loves her so *well.* They're wonderful together, and it makes me so happy for her. She was so sad and lost after losing her mom. And then, last year, when she went to New Orleans to help out with that mess, I thought we might lose her altogether. But we didn't, and then Jonas came, and it's like I have the old Lucy back. I'm so grateful for that."

"You're so sweet," Giles whispers.

"I just love my family."

He leans over and kisses my forehead. "I know you do. You should get some sleep, my love. There shouldn't be any nightmares tonight."

"I can't wait to tell the others tomorrow." I let my eyes flutter closed. "We did good, Giles."

"Yes, baby. We did damn good."

The phone rings.

"Hello?" I haven't even opened my eyes yet as I press the cell to my ear.

"I don't know where Xander is."

"Lorelei?" I crack one eye open and check the time. "It's six in the morning."

"I know. I'm telling you that Xander is missing, Breena. Wake up, for the goddess's sake."

"I was up late." I sit up and brush my hair out of my face. I glance over to look for Giles, but he's already out of bed. "How do you know that Xander is missing?"

"I went to his house this morning," she admits softly. "I've been worried about him, even though he doesn't deserve my worry, and I decided to go check on him. But he's not there. I don't think he's been there in a few days."

Giles walks into the bedroom wearing a pair of gray sweatpants slung low on his hips and carrying two mugs of steaming coffee. My mouth goes a little dry.

Good goddess, he's delicious.

"Breena," Lorelei says into my ear, sounding more annoyed. "Did you go back to sleep?"

"No, sorry. Giles brought me coffee. Did you try simply *calling* Xander? He'd probably answer for you."

"Of course, I did. It immediately went to voicemail as if his phone is dead or turned off."

I frown and look at Giles, putting the phone on speaker. "Lorelei can't find Xander."

"Yeah, something's off," Giles agrees. "I'm going over there."

"I'm here now," Lorelei informs us. "But I can't get inside."

"I have a key," Giles says. "We'll be there shortly."

"Hurry. I'm seriously freaked out." She disconnects, and I sip my coffee.

"It's too early for this." I sigh. "Especially after last night."

"I think we'll all feel better when we find Xander," Giles says. "I can go over by myself if you want to try to get some more sleep."

"No, I'll come with you. I'm worried, too. It's not like Xander to go MIA."

We both dress and finish our coffee, then walk out to the car to drive over to Xander's house.

Lorelei is sitting on the porch, a frown creasing her beautiful face as the early spring breeze flutters the material of her green jacket.

"I'm going to kill him," she announces when I get out of the car. "For making us worry like this."

"There might be a perfectly good explanation," I remind her as Giles unlocks the door, and we step inside.

"Xander?" Giles calls out. "I have Lorelei and Breena with me. We're worried, so we came in."

Lorelei is still, and I can tell she's reaching out through the house with her mind.

"There's no one here," she says at last.

"It feels empty to me, too," I add.

"You two stay down here. I'll go up and look, just to be sure."

Giles climbs the stairs two at a time, calling out for Xander the whole while.

"Where does his father live?" I ask Lorelei. "That's the last time we saw him—when he was talking about his dad."

"I'm not sure," she replies, rubbing her hands over her face. "I think...the last time I remember him mentioning anything, he said his dad lives in Maine somewhere."

"So, not too far away."

"No, just a decent road trip. Or a flight for Xander."

"Maybe he went to find his dad, it went really well, and they've been talking and catching up this whole time," I suggest, but Lorelei only stares at me like I've lost my marbles.

"It's a nice thought, but I highly, *highly* doubt it."

"He's not here," Giles says as he comes down the steps. "The lights that were on last night when we drove by are off now."

"Could they be on a timer?" I ask.

"Maybe, but I don't think so. Of course, I could be wrong."

"Wait." I hold up my finger as inspiration strikes. "You guys, doesn't Xander's family still own an abandoned house over in Danvers? Near the Salem Village Parsonage where the witch trials began?"

"Yeah, it's a historical site, and Xander's family did own a house over there," Lorelei says, thinking back. "It just sat there, empty. Xander mentioned it, but we never went over there."

"We need to find it." I turn to Giles. "Do you know where it is?"

"No, but we can find out. Call Lucy and Jonas to come with us. I have a bad feeling about this."

"On it," I say as I pull out my phone and video call Lucy. "Hey, we think Xander might be in trouble."

"What?" Lucy clears sleep from her eyes. "What's going on?"

"I'll tell you everything, but we think you and Jonas should come over here, to Xander's place. We'll leave from here."

"On our way. Be there in fifteen."

She clicks off, and I turn to Lorelei. "Oh, by the way, we took care of the asshole spirit who tried to kill us. It's gone now."

Her mouth drops open. "What? How? When?"

"I'll explain all of that, too, just as soon as the others get here."

"We destroyed the killer," Breena informs everyone as Jonas and Lucy get out of their car.

"What?" Lucy looks shell-shocked. "Just *now*?"

"No, last night," Breena says and explains what happened with the crystal. "We buried it all over eastern Massachusetts. It's gone."

"Fascinating," Jonas murmurs but doesn't look as if he's ready to celebrate. At least, not yet. "And what's going on with Xander?"

"We don't know." I sigh grimly and look over at his house. "He's not here, and we can't get him to answer any of our calls or texts. It's been several days since any of us has spoken to him, and that's never happened before."

"I think he's hurt," Lorelei says, her voice hushed as if speaking the words aloud will make them true. "I'm *really* scared that he's hurt."

"Okay, we need to find him," Lucy says. "Where would he go?"

"Xander's family owns property over in Danvers, right next to the Old Salem Parsonage."

"Where Samuel Parris lived?" Jonas asks. "Where the hysteria began?"

"That's right," I confirm. "I know the property has been in Xander's family since before the hysteria started."

"I can confirm that," Jonas agrees. "Although the house from three hundred years ago is surely long gone."

"It is," Breena confirms. "But others have been built and torn down since then. No one has lived on the property in about thirty years, and it's sat empty. It's the only place we can think of where Xander might go."

"It's worth checking out," Lucy replies. "What's the address?"

"We don't know." I drag my hand down my face. "But there should be public records."

"I know how to find it," Lorelei says, pulling her phone out of her pocket. "So, I have some neighbors that drive me crazy, and I wanted to find out who they were so I could contact them. There's an app—"

"Of course, there's an app," Lucy mutters.

"—that tells you who owns each property. It was originally made as a hunting app so hunters could contact the owners of properties to get permission to hunt there, but obviously, people use it for all kinds of things." She pinches the screen and narrows her eyes.

"Okay, there's the Old Parsonage of Salem, so I'll just look around that."

She's quiet for a moment and then says, "Aha! Found it."

"Let's go." We pile into my car, and with Lorelei giving me directions, I head into modern-day Danvers, driving as fast as I possibly can on the winding roads. "How much farther?"

"Not far. Turn there, to the right." Lorelei consults her phone. "At the end of this street, you'll take a left. Okay, it should be up here on the right."

The neighborhood is just a regular one, with normal houses set back into the trees. Some look a little dilapidated, and others have obviously been cared for. It's nothing special at all.

But when I find Xander's house, I have to blink several times. "Holy shit."

"Whoa," Breena says from the back seat.

"There's some crazy activity happening in there," Lorelei says. "Also, it doesn't look inhabitable at all. Like, it looks like it's going to cave in at any second."

"Why would Xander let it get this way?"

"It belongs to his father," Lorelei says. "And Xander wants nothing to do with him. As long as his dad's living, it's not Xander's problem."

"Well, let's go see if he's in there," Breena says as she opens the door and hops out.

I hurry after her and grab her arm, stopping her from going up onto the porch.

"Jonas and I will go in."

"Oh, please." Lorelei rolls her eyes. "We have wards on our bodies. Nothing paranormal can kill us, as you well know. We're *all* going in there."

"I forgot," I mutter as I reach into my pocket and wrap my hand around the piece of black tourmaline I brought with me today before glancing at Jonas. "Do you have protection with you?"

"Always," he says with a nod, and we walk to the door.

I turn the knob, and it opens, but when I push it in, something forces me back and slams it shut.

"Something doesn't want us in there," Lucy says.

"Too fucking bad." I push my shoulder against it as Jonas murmurs words of a spell I can't fully understand, and then the door gives, and we shove our way inside.

The floor creaks. Dust floats through the air, and the smell of something that's been dead for a few days permeates the space. It's enough to make my eyes water.

"Please tell me that smell isn't Xander," Breena whispers, clearly terrified that it's exactly that.

"No," Jonas assures her. "It would be far worse than this."

"Look." Lorelei points to the second floor, where we see lights flashing as if a TV is on in the dark. "He's up there."

"We should spread out," I say before she can climb the stairs. "Those steps don't look particularly steady, and we don't need them coming down on us."

We gingerly walk upstairs, single file. The closer we get to the top, the more my stomach roils. I feel sick, and I know we're not going to like what we find up here.

"Oh, my goddess. Xander!" Jonas holds Lorelei back from running to the man.

"Stop," Jonas says into her ear. "You will only hurt yourself right now."

The scene before us is just...horrifying. Xander is sitting on the floor, cross-legged, staring into a mirror. The reflection is not of the room we're in but rather a dimension I don't recognize. Lights swirl, but not beautifully. They're dark, pulsing, and hypnotizing.

"Don't look into that mirror," I instruct the others. And then, very slowly, Xander turns his head to look at us.

He's sweating profusely as if he's trying with everything in him to fight. But his eyes... His eyes swirl with the same colors as in the mirror.

"Go." His voice is guttural, and I know that even just that one word costs him energy in his fight. "Run."

"Xander," Lorelei says again, crying in earnest now. "You son of a bitch, you won't leave me like this. You won't give in to this piece of shit. You fight, do you hear me?"

"He's fighting," Breena says and rubs her hand over Lorelei's back. "What do we do?"

"He tried to do the mirror spell without us," Lucy says, misery in every word. "Damn it, he promised he wouldn't do that."

I glance around the room, trying to gather my wits about me, and then freeze. "You've got to be kidding me. That can't be real."

"What? What is it?" Breena follows my gaze, and then what's left of the color in her face drains out. "That's impossible. We destroyed that thing."

The labradorite flashes in the corner of the room, as perfect as ever.

"Xander's dirty," Lucy says. "It looks as if he was digging holes all night."

"He *followed* us?" Breena demands.

"It has him," Lorelei says, her voice frantic now. "That thing you unleashed last night has Xander and made him dig up the pieces."

"Impossible," Jonas mutters.

Xander lets out a whimper and then throws back his head as if he's being tortured. The anger is swift and fierce as it rolls through me.

"We're going to stop this, right here and now."

"Go," Xander manages to say with another guttural groan.

Instead of running, Jonas raises his hands and begins a spell. The rest of us listen carefully and then join him when he starts it all over again, raising our voices in unison and using all our magic and might to protect Xander.

He yells, sounding in utter agony. And then, before our eyes, he shifts into his crow form. The bird's eyes still swirl with color as he caws and then flies out the window.

The room stills, and the mirror shatters. The crystal loses its flash and then falls into a million pieces on the floor.

"It took him," Lucy says. "Holy shit, it took him."

"We need to leave this place," Jonas says. "It's not safe for us here."

"I need to find Xander." Lorelei leads us down the stairs. When we're all outside by the car, I hear a loud rumble.

We all turn in time to see the house collapsing behind us.

"Let's go." I circle my finger in the air, gesturing for everyone to get the hell inside the car. When we're all safely inside, I peel away from the house and head down the street. "This is absolutely fucking insane."

"Where would Xander go?" Lucy asks Lorelei.

"Xander, or the son of a bitch who has him?" Lorelei counters. "Because as far as that goes, your guess is as good as mine."

"We can't do this alone," I say as I turn toward Salem. "All we did was piss it off. We didn't hurt it. We need the whole coven this time."

"Agreed," Jonas says with a nod. "We need much more magic than what's in this car, and that's saying quite a lot, given how talented we all are."

"We need a plan," Breena adds.

"There's no time for any of this." Lorelei's mood seems to be bordering on hysterical now. "It *has him*. We have to find him and get rid of it, and all without killing

Xander. My goddess, he's in agony. Did you see it? Feel it? It's killing him."

"No," I say quietly, thinking about what I just saw. "It's *using* him. Yes, it's hurting him because it's sadistic and *likes* the torture, but he'll use Xander before he kills him."

"He's going to use Xander to kill *us*," Breena finishes.

"Xander won't hurt me. Not physically. I mean, he destroyed my heart, but he won't physically harm me. I know that. He'd do anything to keep us all safe," Lorelei insists.

"Which is why he was suffering so much in that hellhole," I reply. "Without us. Because he knew it was dangerous, and he was determined to keep us all safe."

I don't stop at my house or any of theirs to drop them off. Instead, I head straight for Astrid and Hilda's house.

"Call the coven," I order as we get out of the car and hurry inside. "Call everyone we know and tell them to get over here."

"Something's happening," Hilda says as she opens the door and embraces Breena. "Are you okay, darling?"

"No. No, I'm not okay. And neither is Xander. We have to call the others. Right now. It's an emergency."

"We need a broken ties spell," Poppy says as she paces the courtyard.

"I don't think burning some twine between two candles is going to do the trick," I reply to my mom.

"Don't discount it," Astrid says, shaking her head. "It can be a very powerful spell, and one that we definitely should have going in the background on this. It's going to take more than one thing to break Xander loose from the hold this spirit has on him. We need to be in teams, working on different spells and incantations at the same time. We have to hit it from all angles."

"She's right." My father looks up from the grimoire he's been studying. "Teamwork is the way to get that thing out of Xander so we can save our leader but also kill the demon."

"Is that what it is? A demon?" I ask him.

"I don't know what else to call it. I don't necessarily believe in demons, devils, or even in hell. But whatever it is, it's pure evil. Pure hate."

"Wait." Breena holds up her hand and stands. "How do we defeat hate?" We all look at her as she looks around the room, meeting everyone's gazes. "With love, of course."

Hilda smiles at her daughter and takes her hand. "You're very sweet, darling, but—"

"It's not about being sweet," Breena interrupts, clearly annoyed. Her mother's eyes widen in surprise.

"I'm not talking about Valentine's Day love here with flowers and pretty underwear. I mean *love*. This thing has so much hate, I think it's actually hate itself, manifested into energy. That energy has the power to move, and killing fuels the energy. That's why it always comes around to kill a witch once a year. For the magic and the energy boost. He turns it into more of his own hate."

"I like where you're going with this," Jonas says. "Keep going."

Breena twists her fingers together as she thinks it over. "It'll be *really* pissed off if we throw a whole bunch of love at it. And I'm talking pure, absolute adoration. I know that we all feel that for Xander. He's our leader. Our friend." She turns to Lorelei. "And he's way more than that for you, even if you don't want to admit it. Even if you won't be with him forever, what you feel for each other is important."

Lorelei shakes her head, but Lucy takes her hand. "Lora, if you didn't love him, you wouldn't be as freaked out as you are right now about what's happening to him."

"I can't love him." She lets out a sob and drops her head into her hands. "It destroyed me once, and I lost everything because of it. I moved on."

"You healed," Astrid says as she rubs her hand over the back of Lorelei's head. "But, my darling daughter, you can't just shut off what *is*. You and Xander are meant for each other. Your bond is an incredibly strong one, even if you don't mate for life. Breena's right. We all love

Xander. And it's going to be our love for him and one another that saves him."

"Unfortunately," my mom adds, "it isn't a quick fix. We have to plan, to prepare. We need shields and wards in place, along with the spell work."

"How much time do we need, Poppy?" Lucy asks her.

"Ideally? A week."

That garners an uproar, and she waves her hands in the air. "Calm down, I said *ideally*. I think we can be ready in twenty-four hours if we don't sleep and work through the night."

"We can do that," Percy says with a nod. "We'll be ready by tomorrow."

"And in the meantime, Xander's just out there somewhere, suffering?" Lorelei shakes her head and wipes tears off her cheeks. "That's absolutely unacceptable. We can't leave him out there in agony."

"Lorelei, we don't know where he is," Breena says, her voice gentle. "We don't know where that thing took him."

"Could they go into Hallows End?" I ask Jonas, and the other man suddenly looks shell-shocked.

"I-I honestly don't know. We know that it was in Hallows End when it inhabited Alistair's body, and that's how it got to Breena. So, I assume it could do that, yes."

"It would make sense for it to hide there," Lucy says. "Hallows End is hidden. We can't get to it there."

"The townspeople wouldn't think anything of a

crow being in town," Jonas adds. "There are crows in Hallows End all the time."

"Then let's go," Lorelei says, but I shake my head.

"We can't just go marching in there," I reply. "We all know that the people who live there would be terrified if a bunch of us just went barging in. They wouldn't understand."

"Can we put them under some kind of a spell?" Astrid asks. "So they don't see us? Perhaps a sleeping spell where they all just sleep right through it."

"Okay, hold on," Percy says. "First of all, we don't know that's where Xander is. Where *it* is. And second of all, that's a whole lot of people to put under a sleeping spell."

"Just under two hundred," Jonas confirms. "But I can go there now and look for him."

"Please, do that." Lorelei reaches for Jonas and holds on to his hand tightly. "Would you please do that right now?"

"Consider it done. I can speak telepathically with Lucy, so you'll know as soon as I confirm one way or the other."

"Thank you." Lorelei offers him a watery smile as Jonas walks away, and then he starts into a jog across the meadow that leads to Lucy's house and the bridge to Hallows End.

"We need to get started on our teamwork," my father says. "Even if we do find him, we'll still need the tools to defeat him. So, let's get to work, everyone."

There are roughly thirty members of the coven present, and they all begin breaking off into groups, immediately discussing plans.

"We work well together," Breena says as she watches the others. "Whether it's for something good like a holiday celebration, or something hard like this, our coven has always worked well together."

"There's a reason it has survived all this time." I loop my arm around her shoulders. "The roots of this coven go back to the days of the witch trials."

"For you and me, they do. But we have newer witches, too, and I think that's important. I like that we aren't snobby."

"I can see that. You're too sweet to be snobby."

A cloud moves over her face, and she turns to me. "Giles, I know my mom was being nice before, but does everyone see me as being a naïve, *nice* girl?"

"Naïve? No. But you *are* nice, and you have a kind soul. You're a pleaser."

"That doesn't make me weak."

"No, ma'am. It definitely doesn't make you weak."

"I'm beginning to realize that people underestimate me, and it's really annoying. I'm a talented witch in my own right."

"I couldn't agree more. I don't think your mother was trying to sound condescending, honey."

"She may not have meant it, but that's exactly how it sounded and came across, and I think I'm done letting people do that to me, even if they mean well.

I'm a smart, successful person. I want to be treated as such."

"As you should. I'm glad you stood up for yourself. A year ago, you might have just laughed and sat down again."

"Maybe. Not anymore. The stakes are too high now, and I'm not the same woman I was a year ago. I've learned too much about myself to go back to being her."

"She's still a part of you." I kiss her head and hug her to me. "But you've grown, too, and that's important."

"Yeah. We're going to defeat this jerk, Giles."

"I hope so. For Xander's sake, I truly hope so."

CHAPTER NINETEEN

If he had known that inhabiting Xander would give him control of all of the witch's gifts, he would have gone this route a long, long time ago.

He can *fly,* soar above Salem and Hallows End, watching the little witches as they go about their daily lives, completely oblivious to the pain and torture he has in store for them.

He can feel the human witch struggling, and he finds it highly amusing. Xander thought he could simply reach into the glass and stop everything that was beginning to unfold... It was laughable.

And now look at him. Completely at the mercy of his every whim.

Flying above the ocean, he looks down and sees the redhead running toward a cottage. The one who's linked to the human he's taken over. He smiles inside with utter glee.

Yes, this is working out wonderfully.

CHAPTER TWENTY
BREENA

I wake with a start, disoriented. But as I look around my mom's living room, I remember I'm with the coven, trying to figure out how to destroy hate.

That's not a thought I imagined I'd ever have.

"You fell asleep." I glance over to find Giles watching me with those amazing eyes that now hold so much concern for me. He pushes his glasses up on his nose, and I smile at him, wanting to reassure him that I'm okay.

"I hope I didn't sleep too long. I have to earn my keep around here."

"Only an hour or so," Lucy assures me. "No biggie. You'll need your strength later."

"We all will."

We spent the night with dozens of books spread out across the house: grimoires, Books of Shadows, diaries, and volumes on crystals and herbs. You name it, we pored over it.

And I think we have a plan for later today.

"It's good that it's not in Hallows End," Lucy says as she reaches for a fresh donut that Poppy made this morning. "The logistics of that would have been a nightmare."

"It's enough of a nightmare as it is," Astrid agrees. "Now that we have everything we need, we just have to *find* Xander—and it."

Many members of the coven went home for a little while to change clothes and gather supplies they would need for their specific tasks. The plan is to meet back here at noon and then move forward with finding Xander, pulling that horrible thing out of him, and then destroying it.

It sounds so simple, but I have a feeling it'll be anything but.

"I'm going to run back to your place to get my cloak and my wand," I say to Giles. "I'll feel better if I have those with me."

"I'll take you," he says and stands, pulling his keys out of his pocket.

"What about Nera and Merlin?" Mom asks.

"What about them?" Lucy replies.

"Should they be alone? This type of warfare is very hard on a familiar."

I worry my lip and look over at Lucy. "Should I take Merlin over to your place to be with Nera?"

"Good idea." Lucy nods in agreement. "Let's do that.

I want to grab a couple of things, too. I think Lorelei already went to her house for some stuff as well. Let's get it all out of the way before we get to work."

"Let's go," Giles agrees.

It's a beautiful spring day in Salem. The sun is already high in the sky, and colorful tulips and daffodils line the fence lines of the little homes in town, giving off the prettiest pops of color.

Giles parks in the drive, and I hurry inside. "Merlin, I'm going to take you to Lucy's to be with Nera today. I don't want you to be scared, okay?"

The cat looks up from the couch, all sleepy-eyed, then stretches long and slow as if he doesn't have a care in the world.

"I think he's okay with it," Lucy replies as I hurry upstairs to the closet.

First, I change into the purple dress I had made. I embroidered magical symbols all over it, and it just feels like *magic*. Then, I pull my cloak off the hanger and drape it over my shoulders.

My wand, made of amethyst and sterling silver, sits on my altar. With that in hand, I turn to hurry back downstairs, but Giles is right behind me.

"You startled me." I grin as he frames my face in his hands and tips his forehead against mine. "It's going to be okay, my love."

"I can't have anything happen to you," he whispers. "I can't lose you now, Breena."

"Hey, you're not losing me. And I'm not losing you

either." I wrap my arms around his middle and cling to him. "We're a strong coven, Giles. We have a solid plan, and we're going to succeed in this. I can feel it."

"I'm going to admit to you, while it's just the two of us here, that I'm terrified. Xander is one of my closest friends, and I didn't like the way he looked yesterday. And if it gets its claws into you again, I could lose you both—"

"Whoa." I hold his face in my hands now. "Stop that. Remember, it *wants* your fear, babe. It wants you to go into this terrified of it and whatever it might do. If you give it that, it's already won."

"You're right." He blows out a breath and then takes another deep one. "You're right. I've just had a few bad moments. I love you more than anything in this world, and I don't want you anywhere near that thing."

"Same goes." I smile and lean in to hug him again. "If I could lock you away in here, I totally would. But Xander needs us both."

"This might sound like toxic masculinity, but the day that you shield me from *anything*, is a day that will never happen."

"That should probably irritate me," I reply, thinking it over. "But it's also kind of hot."

"What do you say we blow off this whole kill-the-monster thing and stay here where I can make love to you all day?"

I grin, glad that he's found even ground again.

"That sounds like a great idea. But unfortunately, we

have to kill the monster. Still, I'll take a rain check on that."

"Tomorrow," he promises and covers my mouth with his, sinking into me. "It'll happen."

"What is taking so long up there?" Lucy calls out.

"On our way," I yell back. "Come on, no more procrastinating." We jog downstairs, where Merlin waits in his kennel next to Lucy's feet.

"We're ready," I announce.

"That dress is *to die for*," Lucy says. "I haven't seen it finished."

"Wow," Giles says, taking in the dress for the first time.

"After what happened at Samhain, I needed something that made me feel powerful when I wore it. I have the ward on my neck, but this holds a lot of power, too. As I embroidered the edges, I worked my own spells and those of my ancestors into the stitches. I think I'm going to need it today."

"I think that's an excellent idea," Lucy says and pulls me in for a quick, fierce hug. "Let's get going. I don't want to miss anything."

It doesn't take long to drop off Merlin with Nera, who's happy to see him. Lucy and Nera have a talk, and the dog hugs her by resting his head on her shoulder.

It's always the sweetest thing I've ever seen.

Then, armed with herbs, her own cloak, and some tools, we make our way back to the coven.

Everyone seems to be back, dressed similarly to us and armed with weapons of their own.

"Where's Lorelei?" I ask, looking around for her.

"She wasn't with you?" Astrid asks.

"No, she left before us. Didn't she go home to get her stuff? She should be back by now."

"I haven't seen her all day," Lucy says, and when I look over at her, I get a sinking feeling in the pit of my stomach. "Oh, no. She wouldn't."

"I'm afraid she would."

"I just found this," my mom announces, hurrying out of the house. "I think Lorelei has done something foolish."

She's carrying a silver tray with a crystal ball and a note on it.

Loved ones,

I can't leave him out there alone. I've gone to look for him. I'll reach out to you when I find him. Don't worry, I have my ward, and I will be careful. I love you, and I'll see you soon.

-L

"I'm going to wring her neck," Lucy grumbles. "Why did she leave it by the crystal ball?"

"So we could find her, of course," Astrid says with tears in her troubled eyes. "My girl is no dummy."

"I can't believe I didn't notice when she left," I mutter, mentally kicking myself. "I should have known she'd try something like this. I should have stopped her."

"It's not helping her or anyone for you to beat yourself up over this now," Mom says. "Let's concentrate on finding her and getting to her before she gets hurt."

Astrid loosens her gaze and focuses on the sphere.

"Do you see her?"

"She's in her house," Astrid says and then goes very pale. "And she's in trouble."

"Let's go," Giles says, his face set in grim lines and looking every part the fierce warrior he is. "It looks like we're starting earlier than planned."

"Lucy and I are going in," I announce when we get to the house by the shoreline. The rest of the coven takes their places around the cottage and on the shore, placing crystal grids, setting out candles for spells, and drawing sigils and runes in the sand. "We're warded, and we're the closest to Lorelei."

"If you think I'll stand idly by while my wife confronts a monster, you're very much mistaken," Jonas says, not unkindly but very sternly. "You may lead, but I'll be there with you, every step of the way."

"Same goes," Giles says, watching me, his jaw set. "I'm not leaving you. All four of us go in together."

"There's no time to argue," Lucy says and takes my hand. "We stand together, and we stand firm. We show no fear. It *wants* our fear. That fuels the hate. Just remember that. Use your anger and your power for what fuels *you*."

I nod, reach for the door, and turn the knob. Then, all of us walk inside.

The energy is palpable. It pulses around us in a sick song of death and destruction.

"She's in the bedroom," Lucy says, and we hurry that way, then stop at the door. The view before us brings us up short.

Lorelei is tied to the bed and only wearing her underwear and bra. She's writhing, her skin drenched in sweat.

Xander stands over her, holding a long knife.

"You won't kill her."

He turns at the sound of my voice. His eyes are still swirling with that horrible light we saw before, and his lips twist into a sick smile as if what I just said is the funniest thing he's ever heard.

"All of you," he hisses. "I will kill *all of you.*"

"The crystal grid is set in the sand, and the others have begun," Giles murmurs from behind me. "Let's do this."

Xander raises his hand above Lorelei's body and makes a fist. She twists, writhing in pain.

"We call on the wind," we begin in unison and work our way through the spell. At first, Xander's face splits back into that awful, sinister smile, but as we continue, and I feel the energy coming from the others outside, from around their cauldrons and crystal grids, with their herbs and oils and sigils, the expression falls.

He doesn't use the knife, but with the slash of his

hand, Lorelei's body bows and then falls, seemingly lifeless.

But we don't stop. I can see that we're battering him. His body jerks and flails until he shifts into his crow form and flies out the window.

We follow, and as we do, Astrid and Mom hurry into the house to see to Lorelei.

The rest of the coven follows us, chanting the spell we devised over and over again. Suddenly, the crow falls out of the air and into the water with a much bigger splash than expected.

Several seconds later, Xander surfaces, back in his human form, but his eyes still swirl, though not as brightly as before. It seems to be dimming, and with that realization, we continue the spell in earnest.

I hear generations of witches around us and feel the power coming off them in waves as we batter the thing inside Xander.

It's a delicate balance of killing the hate but saving the man. Then, suddenly, I hear Lorelei's voice from behind us. She's not chanting the same spell. Instead, she's helping to move our power forward into the water, using her own words.

It's amazing to watch the water churn with her force, to witness it bend to her will. She didn't bother to dress, so she stands with that wild, dark red hair billowing around her, her body tight with fierce anger and pure will, throwing everything she has at it and adding her intention to ours.

"You will not torture the man I love, today or any day. You have no authority here. I call on the sea to strengthen the other half of me, to give him the courage to battle that which holds him prisoner."

She begins to move her arms in a big circle, and the biggest wave I've ever seen in my life forms behind Xander, blocking out the sun. Black clouds form overhead, and Lorelei's green eyes shine as if they're on fire.

The force is inspiring, and the rest of us feel emboldened by her intensity. Our words grow louder, the crystals in the sand glow, and as the wave crests higher over Xander's head, ready to take him under, thunder crashes all around us.

Xander's eyes clear.

We hear another scream, like the one that Giles and I heard when we broke the crystal, but now it's ten times louder and way angrier than before.

Lorelei calms the ocean, and it settles down, the waves not washing over Xander, who's standing in the water, trying to catch his breath.

The swirls of light are out of his eyes, gone and in the ocean now, drifting on the ripples of the waves and moving away from the man we fought so hard to save.

His gaze finds Lorelei, and his expression softens.

"My love." That's all he says before he sways and then falls into the water.

"Hurry, he'll drown!"

"Don't touch the water," Lorelei shouts. "It's still in there. It could take over any of us."

"He's face-down," I remind her, watching as her eyes search the bubbling sea.

Suddenly, Xander flips over onto his back, and I see a fin come out of the water before heading away.

"Was that a *shark*?" Giles asks. "Holy Poseidon, you really are a sea witch."

But Lorelei doesn't smile. Her gaze is firmly fixed on Xander, who still isn't showing any signs of life.

"How do we get him out?" Percy demands. "We can't just let him float out there."

"The light is dissipating," I say, pointing. "It's almost gone."

"I'm going to touch the water," Giles says. "If I suddenly act crazy, please, by all means, knock me the hell out."

He gingerly reaches out to touch the water and then shakes his head. "It's gone. There's nothing here."

"He's right," Lorelei says and lets out a whooshing breath as she and Giles scramble into the water and grab Xander, pulling him toward the shoreline.

Once he's on the sand, Giles touches Xander's neck, checking for a pulse. Suddenly, Xander wakes up, sitting and reaching for Lorelei, pulling her down onto his lap and then burying his face in her neck.

"I'm so sorry. I'm so fucking sorry."

CHAPTER TWENTY-ONE
GILES

"I s it really gone?" my mother asks with wide eyes, holding my dad's hand tightly. "Are we sure?"

"It's gone," Xander says as Lorelei untangles herself from his lap, allowing him to stand. I can see that he wants to reach out for her again, to hold her to him, but she's already shut him out.

It's painful to watch.

"Here," Breena says as she wraps Lorelei in her cloak. "You have to be cold."

"Bone-deep," Lorelei confirms as she pulls the heavy fabric around her. "Thanks. It's a good thing I'm not shy about my body, or I'd be pretty embarrassed right now."

"I think we should get Lorelei inside," Lucy says as she reaches for Jonas's hand. "And get everyone settled."

"We're going to leave you be," Percy says with a kind smile. "Since we're finished here, we'll let the eight of you go inside, and the rest of us will get this all cleaned up. We'll see you at the Beltane celebration."

"Thank you," Xander says, looking at everyone with deep gratitude and emotion in his dark eyes. "I can't express to you how grateful I am that you helped me."

"We're your family," Hilda replies and walks into Xander's arms for a hug. "Of course, we'd fight for you, sweet boy."

"We love you," someone else calls out.

"I love you all, too."

I hang back as Breena and her cousins, their mothers, and Jonas and Xander go inside. I want a moment with my parents.

"Thank you," I say to them. "You were both pretty badass."

"Oh, darling, that thing didn't know what it was up against." Mom kisses my cheek. "Now, go. Be with your girl and your extended family. We'll talk soon."

I nod and walk into the house, seeing that Lorelei has already changed into sweats and an oversized sweatshirt, the hood pulled over her head. She's sitting with a mug of tea in her hands, the spoon stirring without any human help.

Everyone seems to be talking at once, likely because of the adrenaline of the fight and the excitement of victory over something that's been harassing us for so long.

"Your parents could have joined us," Breena says as

she comes to me and takes my hand. "They're always welcome."

"I think they wanted to spend some time with the others and then head home to rest. We'll see them very soon."

"Xander," Astrid says, and the man looks her way. "I, for one, would like to hear your side of what happened over the last few days."

"I would, too," Lucy says.

Xander steps to the window and watches the water for a long moment. "I was foolish," he begins and then turns back to us, looking at each of us with sorrow lining his face. "I owe all of you the biggest apology and my deepest gratitude, but I'll start with what happened."

"You can come sit," Lorelei offers. Her voice is back to being a little cold toward him, but at least she's being nice.

"I'd like to stand. I sat for a few days straight, so stretching my legs feels good."

He pushes his fingers through his hair and blows out another breath. He looks so *big* in the small cottage. On any other day, it would be laughable.

"It started when I left Astrid and Hilda's house to find my father. I had every intention of speaking with him, whether that be on the phone, or in person if he wouldn't take my call. And, well, he didn't take the call. But then I saw him. He's dead."

"So you saw his spirit?" I ask.

"Yes. I will need to have some conversations with him

later because I don't have all the details, but I know that he's crossed over. He just said that the answers I needed were at the property by the old parsonage. That there were some papers and other stuff there I could use for research."

"Wait a minute," Breena says, holding up her hands. "That sounds like *it* took the form of your father and wanted to trap you."

"I would have thought so, too," Xander says, nodding his head, "but when I got to the house, it was true. I found a filing cabinet in the office on the ground floor that actually had a lot of information in it."

"That house was completely dilapidated and nothing but a crumbling shell when we saw it," I interject, frowning. "There was no furniture, and definitely no filing cabinet."

Xander nods and paces back to the window. "As the hours wore on, once it trapped me, it used the house as energy, making it decay rapidly. Then, when you destroyed the crystal, it made me follow you and dig it all up, then take it back to the house. It put it back together again so it could continue to draw energy from it."

"Okay, back up." Jonas speaks for the first time. "You found the papers and started researching. What next?"

"There was a mirror upstairs, and I got to work. I started some scrying work, then moved into a spell. But then the lights started moving in the mirror, and it completely hypnotized me. I couldn't pull out of it. I sat there, just staring, completely entranced for more than a day. Then, it sent me to dig up the crystal. Once it had that back under its control, that's when things got painful."

"You were in agony when we saw you," Lorelei says, her voice raw.

"I tried to get you to run. I didn't know if it would be able to hold all of you the way it had me, and all I wanted was for you all to get away."

"We weren't going to leave you there to fend for yourself," Breena says. "That's not how this works, and you know it."

"What next?" Hilda prompts.

"I think you know the rest. It knew it couldn't defeat all of you, so it flew away out of that house, and we went to Hallows End."

"I didn't see you," Jonas says, scowling.

"We saw you," Xander replies. "I think it went there to hide. Hallows End is beautiful. It's unlike anything I've ever seen."

"Yes, it is," Breena agrees.

"We stayed there overnight, high up in a tree, resting. At least, I think it was just resting, gaining energy. Honestly, it was a reprieve for me because it wasn't constantly torturing me anymore, so we were both able to build our energy. Then, this morning, we flew out of Hallows End. When we reached the ocean, Lorelei was walking toward her house. It saw her, recognized her, and went for her."

He swallows hard, and sweat breaks out on his brow as he gazes over at her, so much pain lining his face.

"We don't need to talk about that part," she says softly. "Let's just say that *it*—not Xander, but *it*—grabbed me, just after I'd taken off my clothes to change. It slapped me around a bit and then tied me to the bed. I think it enjoyed my screams the most."

"For fuck's sake," Xander mutters and drags his hand down his face. "Lorelei—"

"It wasn't you," she insists. "You would never do something like that, least of all to me. I know that, Xander. And compared to what you went through, well, it wasn't too long before the cavalry came in. They know the rest."

"Are you okay to be here?" Breena asks Lorelei. "After what happened?"

Xander's whole body jerks in a visceral reaction to the question.

"My goddess, Lorelei. It didn't even occur to me that you could lose your *home.*"

"I'm fine." Lorelei holds her hand up, stopping Xander's outburst. "This isn't the same as what happened to Breena."

"It kind of is." Xander's gaze whips to mine, but I shrug. "It's not personal, man. Breena was attacked in her home by a supernatural entity that took over a human body. It's exactly the same thing. Only this time, it took over a body the victim knows."

"I'm no fucking victim." Lorelei's eyes spark with anger, and thunder claps outside.

"She's still riled up," Lucy says helpfully.

"I don't know why it feels different," Lorelei continues. "It should be the same, but the house even feels different than it did after what happened to Breena."

"She's not wrong," Jonas adds. "It does feel different."

"Maybe it's because we actually got rid of that fucker for good, whereas before, all we did was wound the hell out of it. Literally." I wrap my arm around Breena. "If you feel safe here, Lorelei, that's all that matters."

"We'll set fresh wards," Astrid says. "Before we leave, we'll cleanse and charge the protection crystals and smudge the house."

"Thanks." Lorelei doesn't argue. "I love you all. Even you." Her eyes narrow on Xander. "I'm still mad at you, and we'll never be what we were, but I care about you. You scared the bloody hell out of me."

His lips twitch. "I love you, too."

The sound of those words leaving his mouth just come across as sad.

"Let's clean up," I suggest. "Before it gets too sappy in here."

"Good idea." Lucy nods but wipes a tear from the corner of her eye. "Let's clean up after this jerk once and for all."

"I've called you both here today because I need your opinion."

Lucy and Lorelei stand across the counter from me at Gems, both with curiosity in their eyes.

"Okay," Lucy says. "We're both good at sharing our opinions."

"I know." I grin at her and pull a tray lined with black velvet from under the counter. There are four rings resting in it. "You know Breena the best. I'm not a fool, and I'm okay with admitting that."

"You're going to propose." Lorelei's voice goes soft and dreamy as she stares down at the rings. "Oh, my goddess, this is the sweetest thing."

"You know, for someone who can be such a hard-ass, you sure have a soft side," I tell her.

"Breena deserves this," she replies. "And she wants it, and I'm just so happy she's getting it."

"I know it's not as important for witches to have traditional engagement rings," I say, "but gemstones are my business, and it wouldn't feel right if I didn't propose with a traditional ring."

"Breena's more of an old-fashioned kind of girl," Lucy agrees, nodding as she reaches for the two-karat diamond ring set with a halo of rubies around it. "She would love something like this."

"Oh, see, I disagree," Lorelei replies and reaches for a different ring. "This one, with the sapphires and diamonds, is more to her taste."

"Honestly, I don't think you can go wrong with any of these," Lucy decides. "Which I know isn't exactly a ton of help."

"No help whatsoever," I say with a laugh. "But it's good to know she wouldn't hate any of them."

"There's nothing here to hate," Lorelei says. "So, when are you going to do it? On the summer solstice?"

"Beltane," I reply and watch as they both gape at me.

"Giles, we're celebrating Beltane *tomorrow*," Lucy reminds me.

"I know, which is why I need to decide on a ring today."

"What's the rush?"

I blink at Lucy and then laugh. "Are you seriously asking me that? The woman who married Jonas mere weeks after meeting him?"

"Okay, okay, point taken."

"It's a fair question," Lorelei points out.

"I don't want to waste any more time. I know she's it for me, so why not make her mine in every way possible as soon as I can? I want to marry her."

"She's going to be *so* excited," Lucy says, clapping her hands. "I think my vote is still the rubies with that kick-ass rock. But you could give her a candy ring, and she'd be thrilled."

"She loves you," Lorelei agrees.

"Thanks, ladies. For confusing me further on the ring decision."

"You're welcome." Lucy's voice is full of cheer as she

leans over the counter to kiss my cheek. "You've got this. Are you proposing at the festival?"

"Yes."

"Good. We will all want to witness it." Lorelei winks at me. "We'll see you tomorrow!"

They wave and walk out of the shop, and I'm left staring at the four rings. I was hoping there would be one that stood out above the others, and it would be a no-brainer decision.

No such luck.

I suppose I could put them all in a hat and pull one randomly.

But that seems stupid.

I turn to put them back in the safe, when something glitters and catches my attention.

"Oh, I never thought of you." A vintage ring I've had on consignment for the past several months sits in the display case. It still hasn't sold. It's a three-karat oval diamond surrounded by a halo designed to look like a regal crown. The detail is impeccable, and it's all set in rose gold. "This would be gorgeous on her finger."

I know the history of the piece as it came from the original owner and was even in its box from the early nineteen hundreds.

But the best part is, they were a member of the coven family, and I know that Breena would love that little piece of history.

With the decision made, I set the ring in its original

box and tuck it into my pocket, making a mental note to pay Percy for it the next time I see him.

"The flowers are my favorite part of the celebration," my mom says as she loops her arm through mine and walks with me between all the tables with their beautiful centerpieces full of spring blooms. "It's a reminder that the Earth is waking back up from winter and soaking in the sunshine."

"I know this is your favorite." I lean down and kiss her cheek. "And I think you're going to like the little surprise I have planned for later today."

Her eyes narrow on me, and then they go wide. "Oh, Giles."

"You're psychic. I'm surprised you didn't know before I did."

"I guess I didn't think to look. Goddess, this is so wonderful."

"I haven't asked yet. She might say no."

"Not a chance." Mom laughs and then pats my arm. "When are you going to do it?"

"Right now."

I smile down at her and then find Breena, who's sitting with her cousins on a bench in the garden.

"Well, hi there," she says, her face lighting up when she sees me. "I was wondering where you'd wandered off to. Lucy was just telling me that she's going to open up her fence line and add more garden space, which I think is an awesome idea."

"That will be great, but it's not what I want to talk about."

Lorelei and Lucy share a look and then excuse themselves. Breena frowns.

"What's wrong?"

"Absolutely nothing." I can feel everyone gathering around behind me. I know they think they're being inconspicuous, but they're not. And that's okay. If I wanted this to be private, I would have waited to do it at home later. "You're absolutely gorgeous today."

Her frown smooths out into a smile, and her eyes soften. "Thank you."

"Then again, you're beautiful every day." I kneel before her and take her hand in mine. Suddenly, all the nerves I've carried with me over the past few days are gone. I know exactly what I want to say to her. "Breena, you're an exceptional person. I know that you don't always think so, but I do believe I'm going to make it my life's mission to make sure you know, every single day, how amazing you really are."

"Oh." She breathes the word softly, and tears fill her eyes, but I keep talking.

"I feel foolish that I never realized before now how truly perfectly suited we are for each other. I knew that I was pulled to you, but I was stubborn and resisted that pull. Then, when someone"—I flick my gaze to the side where I know Lorelei is standing—"let it slip that you had loved me for a long time, it was as though all the puzzle pieces finally fit into place."

"I was so mad," Breena says, brushing at a tear on her cheek. I laugh.

"I know. But I'm so grateful that it happened because it brought us here. Everything that's happened over the past six months, give or take, has led us right *here*, so I can't wish any of it away, no matter how scary or difficult it's been."

"Yeah," she says, nodding her head.

"I knew that I liked my house before you came to live in it, but it was only once you joined me there that it truly became my home. You and Merlin have breathed life into it, and I can't imagine going back to a time when it was just me rattling around in there with a ghost. I can't fathom not having you by my side, no matter where I am, until the day comes that I'm no longer here."

She sniffs, and I pull the ring out of my pocket. I can feel Percy smiling proudly behind me.

"This ring isn't new, but it's precious, and I think you'll like the story behind it."

"That was Percy's mother's ring!" she exclaims, and more tears fall down her cheeks. "I saw it in the shop, and I might have pined for it a time or two. It's so pretty, and I just loved Mary so much."

I can hear the sniffling from behind me now.

"I didn't know you'd seen it."

She nods, her eyes hungry for the ring, but I hold it back until I've finished saying what I need to say.

"I still have to ask the question."

"Oh, right." She laughs and looks up into my eyes. "Go ahead."

I smile and chuckle along with those behind me. "Breena, love of my life, will you do me the incredible honor of becoming my wife?"

"Of course, I will!" She launches herself into my arms at the claps and cheers of everyone we love. "I thought you'd never ask."

She holds out her hand for me to take, and I slide the ring on.

"I love you," she says and frames my face with her hands. "And I'm so happy."

"Me, too." I kiss her, long and slow. "And I plan to keep you happy for a very, very long time."

"I'll hold you to that."

CHAPTER TWENTY-TWO
BREENA

"I have a hole in my dress." This can't be happening. It just *can't*.

"Where?" Mom circles around me, looking for what I saw. "I don't see anything at all amiss with the dress. It's absolutely perfect."

"There." I point down at the full skirt of the princess-style dress and will my tears to stay at bay. "We have less than twenty-four hours until the wedding, Mom. And that's not on a seam, which means it has to be patched. And how, exactly, do you patch a wedding dress?"

"Hmm," is all Mom says before wiggling her fingers. Right before my eyes, the threads of the skirt magically weave themselves back together, and it's as though the hole was never there.

"I didn't know you could do that." I turn away from the three-fold mirror and stare at my mother in wonder.

"Why didn't I know about that? And why aren't *you* the one making the tapestry?"

"First of all, the tapestry isn't my quest, darling girl. That's yours. And secondly, you don't know all the little tricks I have up my sleeve."

"Well, that's one I'd like to learn. It would make the tapestry go so much faster."

Tomorrow is the autumn equinox, and I've been so busy planning for this wedding all summer that I haven't spent as much time on the tapestry as I'd intended.

"You'll be done with it when it needs to be done," she says. "You're almost there as it is."

"It's just adding the embellishments now," I admit and go back to admiring myself in the dress. "But that seems to be the most tedious part. You're right, though. I'll be done on time. Giles and I aren't taking a honeymoon until after Samhain because we want to focus on lifting this curse. I won't be able to relax and enjoy myself until the people of Hallows End are free, and that whole thing is over with."

"As much as I hate that for you," Mom says as she fits the veil to the top of my head, "I think it's probably smart. You only have five more weeks to wait, and then you'll be able to relax and truly enjoy yourself."

Butterflies fill my stomach when I take in the finished product in the mirror. "I love this dress so much."

"It suits you," Mom says as she stands next to me and admires us both in the reflection. "Your Aunt Agatha is thrilled you wanted to use her veil."

"I'm glad." I smile, but my heart hurts at the thought of Aunt Agatha not being at the wedding. "I loved her so much."

"She's still around," Mom reminds me. "And asking each woman in the coven to embroider a symbol on the veil was such a lovely touch."

"I want to feel like I'm wrapped in their magic," I reply. "And that's exactly what it feels like."

Mom smiles at me in the mirror, and for just a millisecond, it turns into that sinister smile I saw months ago when *it* was still around.

But then it's gone, and Mom's just smiling at me, admiring the dress.

"What's wrong?" Mom asks.

"Oh, nothing." I shake my head. "I'm sure it's just all the stress. It's playing games with me."

"What are you up to after this?" she asks as she takes the veil off my head.

"Well, Lorelei and Lucy asked me to go to the apothecary for a little spa time, and then we're going to make the handfasting cord for that part of the ceremony."

"Oh, I think that's lovely." Mom unzips the back of the dress so I can step out of it. "I think everything is good to go here—all ready for tomorrow."

"Thanks, Mom. Oh, and one other thing. With Dad not here, I'd like for you to walk me down the aisle."

Her head comes up in surprise. "You do?"

"Of course. You have to give me away."

"I'd be honored to give my only daughter away."

I kiss her cheek and then hurry to change back into my clothes so I can get over to Lucy's. "I'll see you tomorrow. Are you *sure* you don't want me to come over in the morning? The florist will be here with the flowers around ten, and there will be tables and linens delivered. There's just so much to do. I can come and help before I get dressed for the ceremony. Giles will, too."

"No, your aunt and I have it covered. Besides, Poppy is also coming to help, and I know other members of the coven will pop in to lend a hand, as well. We've got this covered. You just worry about getting some rest and enjoying your morning. I'll have the dress and everything else waiting for you when you arrive to get ready."

"You're the best." I slide my feet into my shoes and then hurry over to kiss Mom's cheek. "I love you so much."

"I love you, too. Have fun today."

"I will. Thanks again."

I hurry out the back door and see Astrid pruning some of the bushes in the backyard.

"How did it go?" she asks me.

"Everything's all set," I reply with a smile. "It's going to be *amazing*."

"You bet your ass, it will be," she says with a wink. "The wedding of the year, right here. And on the autumn equinox, no less. I can't wait."

"Thanks for all your hard work." I kiss her on the

cheek, the same as I did with my mom a minute ago. "You're just wonderful."

"I love you," she says simply. "We'll do whatever you need."

"And it's the best feeling in the world to know that. I'd better go get pampered now."

"Yes, you'd better. Enjoy it, honey."

I wave, hurry over to my car, and then drive the short distance to Lucy's house. Once I've parked, I get out and walk to the door, but then I stop and frown.

Everything in her garden is...*dead*.

"It's too early for this," I hear myself say. "Lucy's plants bloom well past Samhain."

With a frown, I walk up the back steps and knock on the door before pushing inside. "Hello! I'm here. What's up with your—?"

I stop and then gasp. The inside is in shambles, as if someone ransacked the place, looking for stuff to steal.

"Oh, no."

"Breena?"

I hear Lorelei call out from the shop area and turn to look through the door. When I glance back at the kitchen, everything is normal.

Not one thing is out of place.

"I might need to eat," I mutter as I walk into the shop where my cousins are. "I hope you have food."

"Surprise!"

I jump, startled, and then laugh. "What is this?"

Everyone is here, all the members of our coven, including Jonas, Xander, and *Giles*.

"It's a surprise wedding shower," Lucy says. "Co-ed."

"Oh, this is fun." Giles steps over and dips me back into a dramatic kiss, much to everyone's delight based on all the applause. "Hi there, handsome."

"Hi. I'm not good at keeping secrets from you."

I laugh as he sets me back on my feet, and then I feel a little woozy.

"Are you all right, sweet one?" Jonas asks.

"I think I need to eat," I confess. "I've been busy today and must have skipped out on food."

"Oh, we have plenty of that," Lorelei says. "We have a killer taco bar out back. I'm surprised you didn't see it. We thought you'd come through the front door."

I frown over at her. "Really? Out in all the dead plants?"

"Dead plants, my butt," Lucy says, hurrying out back. "Oh, thank the goddess. Everything's fine."

I follow her out and blink in confusion. Lucy's garden is gorgeous and colorful. Thriving.

"Yeah, I need some tacos," I decide as Giles takes my hand, and we walk outside. "This is unexpected and *fun.*"

"Good." He kisses my neck, just below my ear. "You deserve it, my love."

"Are you okay, Breena?" I glance over at Lucy, who's sitting in the seat next to mine, getting her makeup done. I hired hair and makeup for myself and my two cousins, along with the moms.

I thought it would be a lot of fun.

And it has been. We've sipped champagne and laughed, and with our hair finished, we're getting our makeup done now.

"I'm great," I reply.

"You seemed kind of out of it for a minute," Lucy says.

"I think it's just all the excitement," I reply with a shrug. "I swear, I've been seeing weird things over the past twenty-four hours or so. But it has to be stress. I even slept until almost ten this morning, which never happens."

"Maybe it's because we were up so late making that handfasting cord," Lorelei suggests. "It turned out great, but we should have started on that a couple of months ago."

"That could be it," I agree and then take a deep breath.

The truth is, I haven't seen anything off today. Actually, that moment at Lucy's when I first arrived yesterday was the last weird thing to happen. I didn't have any nightmares last night, and I've had a good day today so far.

Maybe I'm just on edge and sensitive to anything odd

because of before.

But I don't need to be. *It's* gone, and the only thing I have to worry about today is enjoying every minute of this wedding before I get back to the loom tomorrow to finish the tapestry before Samhain next month.

So, with that internal pep talk, I let go of the uneasy feeling that yesterday put in my stomach and decide that today is only for happiness.

"Your flowers are *stunning*," Poppy says as she walks into the room, and then she just stops and stares. "Oh, honey, you're *gorgeous.*"

"I don't even have my dress on yet." But I smile and accept the offered hug. "Thank you. How is Giles? I haven't seen him all day, which is so stupid because I don't even believe in old-fashioned customs."

"Really?" Poppy and Mom share a wink. "Is that why you're wearing white and incorporating so many *traditional* things into your day? Because you don't believe in them?"

"Okay, I don't believe in that particular one. Besides, most wedding traditions are based on pagan beliefs."

"True enough. Let Giles get his first look at you when you're dressed," Lorelei suggests. "It'll be a knock-him-on-his-ass moment that he'll remember for the rest of his life."

"But can we do it before the ceremony? So it's a special moment for just the two of us?"

"This is your day," Poppy says. "Of course, you can.

You get dressed, and I'll let Giles know. Where do you want to meet him?"

"Hmm." I purse my lips, thinking it over. "On the south side of the house, where the sun hits that sweet little arbor that Dad built right before he passed away."

"I think that's lovely," Astrid says with a nod. "Just so lovely."

"My mom isn't one to cry much," Lorelei says, passing her mom a tissue. "But she's all weepy today."

"It's hormones," Astrid insists.

"Oh, please, those days are way past," Mom says with a laugh. "It's okay to be a little weepy on a day like today. One of our girls is getting married."

Astrid dabs at her eyes, and I join my mom by the mirror.

"Here we go," I whisper as I let my robe fall to the floor. Mom holds the dress for me to step into, then zips up the back and sets the veil on my head.

When I turn to face the others, there's a collective gasp and then a sigh.

"Holy shit, you're gorgeous," Lorelei says. "Giles is going to pass out cold."

"I hope not." I laugh and take one more look in the mirror. Yeah, this was the right choice. A white, princess-style wedding gown with a full veil, and all the beautiful symbols embroidered around the edge of it by women I love and admire.

"He's ready for you. Oh," Poppy says. "Oh, just look at you."

"Okay, you are all really good for my ego." I laugh and accept lots of hugs and kisses and then take a deep breath. "Okay. I'm ready for him, too. But I don't want anyone else to see."

"I've cleared the way," Poppy promises me. "There's no one out there but Giles, on the south side of the house, like you wanted."

"Thank you." I pick up the skirt so it doesn't get dirty and circle around the house. It's a lovely first day of fall, and the trees have just begun to turn colors.

The arbor my dad built is so pretty, with its vines that wind their way up through the wooden slats.

Giles stands under it, turned away from me. His shoulders look so broad in his black suit. His dark hair has just been cut, and I can see by the way he rocks back on his heels that he's a little nervous.

When I'm only a few feet away, I say, "Well, hi there."

He slowly turns around. When he sees me, he lets out a low whistle. "Wow."

"Wow yourself. Are you a GQ model?"

But he doesn't laugh. Instead, he takes a step toward me and rests his hands on my shoulders, taking me in from head to toe.

"I'm one lucky son of a bitch. I don't know what I did right in a past life to deserve this, but I'm so fucking grateful for it."

"You're sweet. I wanted you to see me first. Alone."

"I'm glad. You know, what do you say we have our little private ceremony, right here and now?"

"Oh, that sounds fun. Let's do it."

His lips twitch with humor, and he takes my hands in his, clearing his throat.

"Wait." I reach into the bust of my dress and pull out the handfasting cord. "Let's do this, too."

"What other treasures do you have hidden in there?"

I laugh up at him. "You'll have to wait to find out."

We wind the cord around our clasped hands, and then I look into his gorgeous eyes framed by his dark glasses. I know with certainty that I'm exactly where I'm supposed to be.

"I'll start," he says, but I shake my head.

"Let's do it together."

And so, we do, reciting our handfasting ceremony commitment vows, alternating back and forth.

"May our mornings bring us joy," I begin.

"And our evenings bring peace." He smiles so gently down at me that it almost weakens my knees.

"May our troubles grow few as our blessings increase."

"May the saddest day of our future be no worse than the happiest day in our past."

I can feel the tears welling in my eyes as I say the next line. "May our hands be forever clasped in friendship."

"And our hearts joined forever in love," he finishes.

"I've dreamed of this day for as long as I can remember," I admit to him, here in this sacred place. "But no matter how wonderful I made it in my mind, it was never as good as this. The love I've found with you is so much bigger, so much *more* than anything I could have thought up in my imagination. I'm so honored to be your wife, Giles Corey. I will be faithful to you, I will love you, and I will support you through whatever the universe throws our way until I'm no longer of this Earth."

He swallows hard, and I see tears in his eyes when he moves even closer to me and speaks his vows in such sweet, hushed tones.

"I love you, Breena. With everything in me, with every breath I take, I love you so much that there are times I think I might explode with it. The craziest part is that love just grows each day, and I find that I can hold even more, despite thinking for sure there was no way that could possibly be true. You're everything good in this world. Your compassion, love, and your kindness are treasures, and the way you so effortlessly give those things to others makes me proud—and sometimes a little protective because I want to keep you safe from anyone who might take you for granted. You are my home. You are the best part of every day. I will be faithful to you, I will love you, and I will support you through whatever this wild universe throws our way until I'm no longer of this Earth."

I sigh happily. "I think this means you can kiss me now."

"Hell, yes, it does."

He leans in and presses his lips to mine, gently at first, and then the kiss turns more passionate, *needier*.

When he finally pulls away, I can't help but laugh.

"Maybe we don't recreate that kiss at the official ceremony. We can keep that just for us."

"Good plan." He kisses my hand after we untie the cord. "Let's do this so I can take my wife home and make love to her."

"I'm all for that." I laugh as we walk back toward the house. "The sooner, the better."

Epilogue

He's watching.

Waiting.

They thought they destroyed him, but all they succeeded in doing was dispersing the energy and injuring him for a little while.

He's had time to heal, to hoard the power that grows, and to feed on the anger and absolute rage that fills him each time he sees *them*.

A wedding? Preposterous. Sure, go ahead and celebrate your pathetic lives. All of them. He will soon remind them who's in charge and how much pain he can inflict on them.

How much death and destruction he can cause.

It's almost time to begin, and he's feeling stronger than ever before. Their joy will be short-lived.

But their pain will last for a long time.

The blood is owed. And he will collect.

He will kill them all.

Are you ready for the conclusion to the Curse of the Blood Moon, Xander and Lorelei's story? You can get all of the info here:

www.kristenprobyauthor.com/salems-song

About the Author

Kristen Proby has published more than sixty titles, many of which have hit the USA Today, New York Times and Wall Street Journal Bestsellers lists.

Kristen and her husband, John, make their home in her hometown of Whitefish, Montana with their two cats and dog.

facebook.com/booksbykristenproby

instagram.com/kristenproby

bookbub.com/profile/kristen-proby

goodreads.com/kristenproby

Newsletter Sign Up

I hope you enjoyed reading this story as much as I enjoyed writing it! For upcoming book news, be sure to join my newsletter! I promise I will only send you news-filled mail, and none of the spam. You can sign up here:

https://mailchi.mp/kristenproby.com/newsletter-sign-up

ALSO BY KRISTEN PROBY:

Other Books by Kristen Proby

The Single in Seattle Series
The Secret
The Surprise
The Scandal
The Score

The Huckleberry Bay Series
Lighthouse Way
Fernhill Lane
Chapel Bend

The Curse of the Blood Moon Series
Hallows End
Cauldrons Call

The With Me In Seattle Series

Come Away With Me
Under The Mistletoe With Me
Fight With Me
Play With Me
Rock With Me
Safe With Me
Tied With Me
Breathe With Me
Forever With Me
Stay With Me
Indulge With Me
Love With Me
Dance With Me
Dream With Me
You Belong With Me
Imagine With Me
Shine With Me
Escape With Me
Flirt With Me
Change With Me
Take a Chance With Me

Check out the full series here: https://www.
kristenprobyauthor.com/with-me-in-seattle

The Big Sky Universe

Love Under the Big Sky

Loving Cara

Seducing Lauren

Falling for Jillian

Saving Grace

The Big Sky

Charming Hannah

Kissing Jenna

Waiting for Willa

Soaring With Fallon

Big Sky Royal

Enchanting Sebastian

Enticing Liam

Taunting Callum

Heroes of Big Sky

Honor

Courage

Shelter

Check out the full Big Sky universe here: https:// www.kristenprobyauthor.com/under-the-big-sky

Bayou Magic

Shadows

Spells

Serendipity

Check out the full series here: https://www.
kristenprobyauthor.com/bayou-magic

The Romancing Manhattan Series

All the Way
All it Takes
After All

Check out the full series here: https://www.
kristenprobyauthor.com/romancing-manhattan

The Boudreaux Series

Easy Love
Easy Charm
Easy Melody
Easy Kisses
Easy Magic
Easy Fortune
Easy Nights

Check out the full series here: https://www.
kristenprobyauthor.com/boudreaux

The Fusion Series

Listen to Me
Close to You

Blush for Me
The Beauty of Us
Savor You

Check out the full series here: https://www.
kristenprobyauthor.com/fusion

From 1001 Dark Nights

Easy With You
Easy For Keeps
No Reservations
Tempting Brooke
Wonder With Me
Shine With Me

Kristen Proby's Crossover Collection

Soaring with Fallon, A Big Sky Novel

Wicked Force: A Wicked Horse Vegas/Big Sky Novella
By Sawyer Bennett

All Stars Fall: A Seaside Pictures/Big Sky Novella
By Rachel Van Dyken

Hold On: A Play On/Big Sky Novella
By Samantha Young

Worth Fighting For: A Warrior Fight Club/Big Sky
Novella
By Laura Kaye

Crazy Imperfect Love: A Dirty Dicks/Big Sky Novella
By K.L. Grayson

Nothing Without You: A Forever Yours/Big Sky Novella
By Monica Murphy

Check out the entire Crossover Collection here:
https://www.kristenprobyauthor.com/kristen-proby-crossover-collection